The Fed Anthology

The Fed Anthology

Edited by
Susan Musgrave

ANVIL PRESS | VANCOUVER | 2003

NATIONAL LIBRARY OF CANADA CATALOGUING IN PUBLICATION DATA

The Fed Anthology: brand new fiction and poetry from the Federation of BC Writers / edited Susan Musgrave.

ISBN 1-895636-48-5

1. Canadian literature (English)—British Columbia. 2. Canadian literature (English)—21st century. I. Musgrave, Susan, 1951- II. Federation of BC Writers.
PS8255.B7F39 2003   C810.8'09711   C2003-910174-6
PR9198.2.B72F39 2003

Printed and bound in Canada
Jacket by Typesmith Design
Typeset by HeimatHouse

Represented in Canada by the Literary Press Group
Distributed by the University of Toronto Press

The publisher gratefully acknowledges the financial assistance of the BC Arts Council, the Canada Council for the Arts, and the Book Publishing Industry Development Program (BPIDP) for their support of our publishing program.

Anvil Press
6 West 17th Avenue
Vancouver, BC V5Y 1Z4   CANADA
www.anvilpress.com

Table of Contents

Note

During the autumn of 2002 there was an interesting debate in *WordWorks*, the quarterly journal of the Federation of BC Writers, as to whether the group was celebrating its 20th anniversary or its 25th; each side offered documents and recollections in support of its position. I found this an amusing proof of the Fed's spirit and creative ungainliness: just what you might expect of an organization made up of a thousand writers, of every conceivable type, scattered throughout the province from the US border to the Yukon. *The Fed Anthology* is another such illustration.

When I became the Fed's president for 2002-03, I suggested it was high time that someone publish an anthology to showcase the range and diversity of work by members of the Fed, which includes both established and emerging writers. We put out a call for poetry and very short fiction, thinking to include other genres in later years if the response was encouraging. Well, it wasn't just encouraging, it was overwhelming. Michael Armstrong, the Prince George poet and actor who is the Fed's immediate past president, bravely and perhaps foolishly agreed to read what he foresaw as the modest pile of incoming manuscripts. He received, quite literally, thousands of pages from hundreds of members. He and three northern colleagues—Gordon Long, Dominic Maguire and Al Rempel—read and discussed them all, passing along the cream to the distinguished poet and novelist Susan Musgrave on Vancouver Island. From this stack, itself far taller than we had imagined the original total would be, she made the selection you see here, often working with the individual writers to hone and refine their contributions.

The feedback has shown us that a *Fed Anthology* should probably be an annual rite, joining the Fed's other initiatives such as its yearly writers' conference, its cabin-in-the-woods writers' retreat and its professional development classes for published writers. For details as they emerge, please check the Fed's website (www.bcwriters.com).

George Fetherling
Vancouver, BC
January 2003

Foreword

Years ago my friend the writer Marilyn Bowering entered her newborn daughter in a Beautiful Baby contest at the Sooke Fall Fair on Vancouver Island. The judge, a local doctor, poked and prodded and stretched the baby's tiny legs as if she were a Thanksgiving turkey being tested for doneness. The whole process of submitting our work for publication and making, or not making, short-lists has turned into a kind of ugly contest. It hurts to see our offspring graded and categorized so that they can be sent to the market for slaughter.

Writing used to be subversive, something we did to shake up the status quo. Now with gala black-tie dinners where the hors d'oeuvre are worth more than most writers' houses, it has *become* the status quo. We writers need to take back not just the night, but the world. The world within the word that has nothing to do with Best in Show or a TV celebrity's quick pick of the moment.

This is one reason I have resisted calling this anthology "the best of the Fed" (although there were over a thousand submissions from members in every region of the province): being best is beside the point. (I once proposed, in the wake of the success of the hardy American annual, *The Best American Poetry*, that an established Canadian publisher bring out *Second-Best Canadian Poetry*, since we are a more humble, self-effacing lot; they loved the idea but didn't think it would "fly.") Another writer, put in my desperate position—being informed, at the end, that I had to drop ten or fifteen excellent poems and stories from an ever burgeoning manuscript—may have picked an entirely different selection of poems and stories.

There have been plenty of "debut anthologies" in the past century as Canadian literature has come into its own. An anthology (the word comes from the Greek *anthos* and means "a gathering of flowers") is an excellent place to start when you want to acquaint yourself with new voices and different writing styles. *The Fed Anthology*, a first for the Fed, offers readers a taste of everything, a chance to smell not only the roses and the night-flowering jasmine but the skunk cabbage and the stinkweed as well (to extend the "gathering of flowers" metaphor, which I am not quite sure I am capable of doing). More plainly put, you'll find writing here that is painfully beautiful and beautiful writing that reeks of painful truths.

What else? There's love, grief, travel, birth, old age, death, sex and two short stories about parrots in between. There is work by emerging writers though I have never liked the term. (*Emerging* makes me think of something you want to fog with RAID, before it bursts out and becomes something invasive that must be aerially sprayed before it becomes pervasive. I looked up emerge in the *Shorter Oxford Dictionary on Historical Principles*: "To rise by virtue of buoyancy from or out of a liquid. To come up out of a liquid in which a subject has been immersed." I will not incriminate myself by speculating on what this might have to do with one's writing life.)

You'll also find work by established writers who have fully emerged and are buoyantly creating some of the best writing in the land. (That last sentence sounds like a line you'd read in an introduction to an anthology by someone who doesn't make a living from writing: the truth is most of us are struggling just to stay afloat, going back down for the third time—not waving but drowning, to crib from Stevie Smith—when the royalties don't pay the rent.)

Of course there are writers in this collection who are somewhere in between emerging and going back down for the third time. If there is anyone reading this who is *not* a writer, it won't encourage them to choose this "vocation of unhappiness" (not my definition, but I won't contest it), will it?

The best thing about being a writer, of course, is that you can work alone. When I was in Grade Eight, and acting up (i.e., writing poetry instead of paying attention in Math) my principal called me to his office and told me that if I kept up my slipping-down life, and didn't matriculate, I'd have no choice but to end my life as a prostitute. Even back then I knew the world's oldest profession was not in the cards for me. I didn't want a job where you had to work with other people.

We may work alone, but then our work finds its way into

the world. This eclectic anthology attests to the vitality of the written arts in British Columbia, with more of our words and stories being brought to the attention of more people than ever before. Read this book for the pure pleasure of it and you will find abundance.

Susan Musgrave
North Saanich, BC
January 2003

LORNA CROZIER

Needles

His house was full of needles,
a few in plain sight, others
hidden between books or under
cushions, and one I found
on the floor of my car he'd borrowed,
lying there beside a Mars bar wrapper,
harmless, I suppose, though it made me cringe.
I threw it out and said nothing to him,
knowing he'd be ashamed.
Such a gentleman he was no matter
what his state, and loyal to his friends.
Now he's gone, I watch his wife in their house
with a different kind of needle in her hand,
the tip blunt, drawing in milk from a cup
to feed the runt of the litter. She hadn't
noticed how small he was and dying
till she caught the mother with him in her mouth,
heading out the door. Watching
the scrawny kitten suck on plastic
I wonder what's the use but I don't say so.
The other four, I know, will be hard enough
to give away. Maybe since her husband left
she needs something close to dying
she can hold in her hand, some
small thing sucking from a needle
that will make him live.

BETSY TRUMPENER

Satan's House

He hands me a tea bag.

It's wet and warm and there's a twig sticking out of it.

He says, This is my testicle.

He says, Keep it for me, willya?

The tea bag bleeds onto my hand. I say, Keith, man, it's time to go. And he says, I mean it. Gotta go to Satan's House to sleep. If they boil it up for dinner, I'm done for. Please.

And Butchie's swabbing down the tables with a rag from the kitchen, heaving up chairs, emptying ashtrays, shouting WHO LEFT THEIR DIRTY MR. NOODLE DISHES OUT HERE, COME ON PEOPLE, WHO'S GOING TO WASH UP!? and no one even turns to look, too busy packing up their blankets and shit into BiWay bags. A squeegie guy's already banging on the door, begging to run his soaking socks through the dryer once, just once, s'il vous plaît, come on, chum. Leisha asking to borrow a loonie or two from me, pay you back tomorrow, got no streetcar ticket to get to Out of the Cold and eat some STEW. Butchie's shouting QUIT DAWDLING, five o'clock, LET'S GO

FOLKS! And this guy, Keith hands me this tea bag, and I'm holding it and it's leaching brown stuff onto my palm and I'm thinking of the henna designs they drew on Mina's hands before she got hitched. And then we're closed and everyone's heading out into the rain.

·⌐

Some of these guys are nasty. Angrier than my father, even. Sit here and simmer. You might be playing euchre and someone will freak out and be like: I said jail rules, ya dumb fuck! And one guy, that friend of Riley's, once waved his pool cue at my head, after I told them to let the girls play— and I hid in the staff office and bawled, sitting on the floor below the windows so no one would see me cry. But Keith's not bad.

I remember once, in Sunday school, a long time ago, they showed us this movie about a clown washing rich people's feet inside a circus tent. And all these people with dirty shoes were laughing and hee-hawing at the clown, until they finally turned on him and killed him. I felt sorry for that clown. I really did. He was just cleaning people's shoes with a brush. He never asked to be crucified.

Last winter, this old guy came in with a woman, and they were looking for coats, so I sent them down to the donations room in the basement. But they took a long time, and when I went down there, they were in there fucking on a pile of dresses, donations from someone's dead grandmother. I had to kick them out, coats or no coats. The guy just shrugged at me. "We got nowhere else to get it on."

I head home through their turf—Hey, Riley, hey, where you sleeping?—to my high-rise apartment with a big old empty bed and lots of square feet. I sit watching TV alone with their smoke in my hair. In the morning, I'm back here, mopping vomit off the front steps in the rain. While I'm swabbing the cement down with bleach, the lady from the gallery across the street stands frowning at me from under her umbrella, sipping on a skinny latte. I want to tell her that Jesus was a homeless baby, but I don't really have the energy, so I just mop.

"Keith trusts you with his balls?" says Butchie, shaking his head and letting out a mouthful of smoke. "Oh, girl!" It's the end of the day, staff meeting time, time to smoke and write down the worst shit of the day in a black book we keep locked in the staff office. Tattle tales.

– T. broke leg; stitches on ankles and knees but hospital won't keep her and no $ for crutches; Butchie will check w/ hospital social worker.

– New woman (cathy?) lost apt, staying with friends, may lose kids

– K. gave Sheryl a tea bag & said was his "testicle"

– R and N helping at reception; maybe doing crack deals on the phone? Yes: bar for two weeks. Aileen will talk w/ them.

Aileen's the boss. She asks if I feel "okay" about Keith handing me something as if it's his testicle. "Well, it's kinda gross," I say. "But I think he's just worried about his stuff getting ripped off over at the hostel. So, whatever. I might as well keep it for him. For safekeeping. I don't mind." "Well," Aileen says, blowing out smoke, "check it out with him. But let him know it's not okay to be saying stuff like that."

The social work placement student writes it down in the book.

– Sheryl will check in with K. about comment; may keep teabag for safekeeping. She re-ties her pony tail.

After the staff meeting, we sometimes go drinking down the street. I don't really drink much, but some of the staff, the ones who've been here way too long, they pour it back until they sob about their own sorry lives. It's a bit much at the end of the day.

After they've ordered another round of draft, the placement student says the nurse told her Keith's been sleeping at the hostel since his operation. Butchie says it's Keith's own damn fault for being such a slut. How come none of us can get laid and Keith is always shacking up and slipping out to go fuck in the alley?

Aileen says that's bullshit. That Keith's been sleeping out all summer in the urinals at Oak Park and couldn't bathe, so the infection couldn't drain and it never healed. That Keith's testicle, swollen big as a grapefruit, is now floating in a formaldehyde bath on the desk of some doctor at the hospital downtown.

Butchie tells me I better get back to work and dig that tea bag out of the trash. "I saw you toss it," he says. "Whatever," I say. "You're on drugs."

One morning, I come in early to make 150 tuna sandwiches for the protest against homeless deaths with that guy who has blisters on his face and I finally feel fine. I open cans of tuna while he toasts and butters three hundred slices of white bread. He tells me his lady friend got fried in her sleep from a steam vent.

Second degree, he tells me. But it's healing pretty good. He sings me a country and western song he wrote. He says he wants to give his lady a good night's sleep, get her a comfortable bed. Right on, I tell him. That's great.

A few weeks later, they pick him up for robbing a bank with her hairbrush.

CAROLINE WOODWARD

Flight Plans

"I won't be making any more airplane trips," Helga Martin announces. "This roof might go sometime. Or maybe I'll get air-conditioning."

I'm trapped, as always, for Viennese coffee and "something sweet to go with it." She's my last appointment of the day, of this entire hellacious week, tracking her blood pressure, working with the diabetes, all her meds, her state of mind. She shoves the crystal serving plate piled high with spicy, buttery cookies ("Mandel Kucha, lots of almonds and cinnamon, you will like to eat?") toward me, waving one chubby arm at the television. She bats imaginary crumbs off the immense glass and oak coffee-table between us.

"Are you okay with that?" I ask. "I thought you planned on one more trip."

Helga is flushed, beads of perspiration stand out on her forehead. One drop rolls down her jaw, gathering a tiny avalanche of sweat, plopping on the coffee-table glass. Helga has two speeds: frantic and full stop.

"Me? Sure, I'm okay!" She shoots me a look that is both

indignant and puzzled before reaching for her own coffee. She takes a big sip of it, her consistently perfect coffee topped with a swirl of whipped cream. She downs a cup in three minutes flat. Helga can be prickly though and very sensitive to real, or imagined, slights. I choose my words carefully.

"About the trip, I mean . . . your sisters in Austria. Would they come here then?"

Her face lights up instantly, her fine, tanned skin creasing into a broad, dentured smile while her lovely china blue eyes radiate joy for just a few seconds. But she sighs and shakes her silver head.

"Not possible," she says, looking down. "Ella's husband is no good, has that kind of cancer that drags on for years. She can't leave him and Katya is a little . . . you know?" She taps the side of her temple twice and stops, staring in mid-air. "Alzheimer's," she finally says, and nods with a little half-smile and a shrug.

For once I haven't rushed in to finish her sentence while she rummages around for the correct English word. Especially this word.

"No, she is managing fine in the special home over there but travel on a plane all the way to Canada . . . no."

"But didn't you enjoy your trips back home? Seeing the mountain flowers, going up to your family's village?"

I feel safe mentioning these because she had shown me dozens of rather good photos from her visit two years ago. All three silver-haired sisters beaming happily for the cameras high above Innsbruck.

"Yah. But I have seen it all now." She takes half a cookie in one fast bite and starts talking. I have to look down.

"And my sisters, cough, they know, cough, cough, cough. Ach, Gott!" She rushes out to her kitchen and I hear the water tap turned on full blast. Then she rushes back to the living room, apologizing as always, for crumbs going down the wrong pipe. She is 74 and she will never stop talking with her mouth full of food. She says she only eats cookies with me "so I can check up on her easy" but she is kidding herself and fooling nobody, despite being all agog at the test results every week. She is a fantastic baker, to make matters more difficult.

"Anyway, my two sisters, all I have left over there, I have seen now four times in the last twelve years. So that's enough, heh? Good visits, all of them very nice."

I nod silently, maintaining my calm, professional demeanour, and start drinking from my own elegant glass cup at last. I think about the drive I face through early rush-hour to the squat five-story concrete block which houses my office and that I need to finish my month-end report this afternoon or else get to work at 6 a.m. on Monday morning.

Helga is yelling something. I set my cup down too quickly and slop hot coffee on my right hand. She has forgotten serviettes, not at all like her, so I slide my dripping hand down the side of my navy pants. She is pointing at the TV, thankfully muted during our session, but I can see the replay of the jets slamming into the Towers and the fleeing ash-covered secretaries. Then the firefighters and the stretcher-bearers and all of it, all over again, spooling onward relentlessly. Helga wants the remote control. I see it beside her phone, grab it and turn the thing off.

"See!" she hollers. "You never know what nut is getting on the plane with you. No, I'm staying put!"

"Don't blame you at all, Helga," I say, worrying about her purpling face. "May I have some more of your good coffee, please?"

"Yes! My goodness, yes, of course. Here, let me do that."

Handily distracted by the priorities of hospitality, she insists that we look at her photographs in two heavy burgundy cloth-covered albums, page after page from the 1920s to the early '50s. I notice that Helga is astonishingly beautiful, as hollow-cheeked as a model, with a coltish, gaunt figure.

"Oh, yah," she says when I tell her how beautiful she is, "But too skinny, heh? We just about starved, hungry all the time. No meat, only some root vegetables, bread on rations, milk also, no fruit. I missed fruit so much."

We sit side by side on her chesterfield, looking at the clusters of smiling children at the seaside, the three beautiful, bony, young sisters handing down their best dresses to each other, now plump, debilitated old women slowly losing their minds and their bodies an ocean apart from each other.

I stay with her a half-hour longer than I'd intended and then make my way out to my car. Helga has the diet sheets magnetized to her fridge door and has followed my whole spiel, nodding vigorously all the while. Will she stop eating so much of the wrong food and turn the TV off to go for brisk walks, never mind swimming laps or taking up tai chi? Not any time soon. Now I will have to work later just to finish up today's paperwork, never mind the month-end report.

Tonight one of Will's professor pals is hosting a department party for two new instructors. We have to go. I'd rather do my paperwork.

.⌣

I manage a four-minute shower and scramble into one of my two evening semi-formal outfits, what Will calls my Velveteen Bunny suits. I swig the glass of U-Brew Pinot Gris he hands me as I fly between the bathroom and the bedroom, yanking on the velour pants and the matching indigo tunic. My pretty silver-spangled scarf from Will and long silver earrings from my own lovely sister complete the ensemble. I would do almost anything to order in from Rajah's and watch a video with Will, sipping our own not-too-bad cheap wine.

I crave our quiet weekends at home, the long beach walks with Clancy running and sniffing, performing as Completely Ecstatic Mutt. Will is a good man, a dab hand at the omelettes, cuddly and sweet in bed, which is especially heavenly every Saturday morning when we spend hours reading our three papers side by side, drinking his excellent coffee.

This is likely Will's second-to-last academic position. I keep mum, maintaining my agreeable partner-of-prof persona. I nurture the small interior glow induced by the Pinot Gris as Will drives across town and hope for a houseful of guests at our destination. Once upon a time there had been lots of lively grad students way beyond calculated kissing-up to senior faculty, renegade women cutting loose on the dance floor, the sweet scent of sinsemilla wafting in from the Craftsman-style decks.

Roger and Shelagh live in a condo at the outskirts of the city. I am trapped at a coffee-table again. One filled with saucers of peanuts and pretzels, no generous mound of spicy almond cookies or overflowing fruit bowl. There are only nine people here and apparently, that's all there will be. I look around for Marisa but she's not here either. Will accepts two glasses of wine from our host and the two new instructors, both incredibly young-looking women, are introduced. Will leans toward my ear as Roger bustles into the kitchen.

"Vital information," Will hisses. "Shelagh's left Roger."

Roger returns to the huddled circle and soldiers on in the conversation department, extolling the city, the campus, the department. I remember Shelagh once said he was too used to giving fifty-minute lectures whether it was while shopping at a neighbourhood deli or booking an oil change at Canadian Tire. I contemplate a second, no, make that a third, glass of wine this evening when he finally grinds to a halt. He looks around, inspecting glasses.

"More wine? Pretzels? Marvin, you go for those pretzels, don't you!" He hurries back into the kitchen and there is an awkward lull. I catch the two new instructors giving each other a sidelong glance of commiseration and Harvey makes no bones about looking at his watch.

"Well, enough of the pep squad. Let's talk about today, tonight! Anybody stun themselves silly watching television?" A barking sound follows.

It's Rudy, the one Will says cokes up before lectures. He

certainly has a glint in his furtive little eyes tonight. Will
also claims he is a functioning sociopath.

"I thought about running it as backdrop in my classes but
hey, gotta curb anything remotely controversial these days.
Like we're all gonna shed tears for a bunch of dead stock-
brokers, huh?"

He sits back grinning, reaches for the dusty peanuts and
starts tossing them high in the air, trapping them in his glis-
tening open mouth.

Molly Bingham starts braying on cue. Will calls Rudy and
Molly the Gruesome Twosome of the department, Cain and
his Enabler, I Move and I Second, on and on, ad nauseam.
Now she is saying something about the death of irony and
he is interrupting and yelling no, no, say it ain't so and they
are performing a dialogue for us all now and my ears fill up
with a jumble of surf and mercifully blot them out.

One of the instructors, Gloria Al Fayed, the tiny dark-
haired one, is frozen in place, staring at the glass of water
she is holding. The others are all tittering like intellectuals
at a corn roast except for Will whose gaze is fixed morosely
on the carpet between his feet. Which has a small piece of
pizza crust and white cat hair clumps on it.

Roger's head appears around the corner of the kitchen, a
phone affixed to his ear, and his kind, round face lights up
at the sound of his guests enjoying a good joke, he'd have
to enquire later but all was not lost, his guests on this awful
day when his wife finally made good her threats were hav-
ing a normal group chuckle.

I wonder if I could run them both down with my little
blue nurse car, a mid-size compact, if that would do the job.

I wonder if I would back up for an instant replay to ensure the squashed Ass of Irony and his bloody-minded sycophant. Will taps me on the knee and we nod in unison, setting our glasses on the table.

Will is gracious as we make our exit. I trust myself only enough to keep silent. Roger is still on the phone when we step out into the cool, sweet air of early autumn.

"Let's not even talk about it," I say. "Let's not ruin what's left of this evening, if you don't mind."

"Not at all, happy to leave that lot behind us," he says, winking, opening the door so I can sink gratefully onto the seat beside him. I put Telemann's Twelve Fantasias for Flute into the CD deck and the beautiful breathy notes spool around us. I close my eyes and think of the vast expanse of the grey-green Atlantic, endless rolling watery trenches and a tiny silver plane hurtling into a livid orange and purple bank of cloud just off the continent.

And I see Helga Martin, longtime widow, clutching a formidable handbag, wearing one of her ample pastel leisure suits, perching on the edge of her seat, eyes closed, praying or perhaps counting silently, trying so hard not to hyperventilate, to just stay calm, to hang on until she can spot their familiar faces in the crowd.

LAURA J. CUTLER

The Implosion

I moved a lot of mountains to create my cocoon. I thought. I quit my job as a Welfare Act policy writer for the provincial government. I prostrated myself for a cabin: friends' of friends' of friends'. I kissed good-bye, literally and figuratively, a husband of twelve years. Okay, technically, he'd been gone for a month already, but it sealed things, to announce that I was leaving the city for an indeterminate amount of time.

And yet, I am sitting now on an ancient sun chair, the kind with the scratchy reams of interwoven plastic strips, drinking Hochtaler wine from a metallic blue tumbler and thinking about the fallibility of life, cocoons or not.

Abe, my wanna-be, encicingly endowed lover—so he says—called at one-thirty to firm up plans to visit me. In my cocoon. I hemmed and hawed. I didn't want my papery cover pierced; I didn't know how to ask that it not be. I said things like, "I might not stay for the weekend, after all." I said, "I might relocate to Tofino; I'm not happy with the cabin." This latter excuse is an utter lie. The cabin is stocked and cozy. It has exactly the right amount of conveniences, without being anything remotely like modern. I need basics in my life at this juncture: water, wine, maudlin silence.

After I manipulated a fresh twenty-four hours of solitude—until he calls and begins his assault campaign again tomorrow—he gasped and said, "Good God, I must tell you. Have you had the news on?"

"No." I glanced at the bulky old ghetto blaster on top of the fridge and felt my face scrunch up—at the thought of intrusive radio waves or too much September sun, I didn't know.

"Prepare yourself," he cautioned. I was sitting on the front stoop of the cabin, watching dogfish leap and belly flop in the strait. In fifteen minutes, the afternoon sun would kiss my sandaled toes, wrinkly knees, belly, pale nipples, shoulders and lastly, my lugubrious face: this is what nature would have bestowed on me, natural golden kisses.

"The US has been attacked by terrorists," he continued gravely. "Big time. The World Trade and Convention Center, in New York. Hijacked planes flew into them."

"You're kidding," I responded automatically, what he was saying seriously prodding, but not yet bursting, my cocoon.

"It's huge," he assured. "And the Pentagon, same idea. A fourth plane seems to have been deliberately crashed in Philadelphia. Pittsburgh. Pennsylvania. A 'P' place. You need to turn on the news. Do you have a TV there?"

"No," I answered honestly. "A radio."

"You need to tune in."

"Who, who is responsible?" I pressed, though I really

wished he hadn't told me anything at all. My silky balloon lies around me in deflated folds.

"They don't know yet. Terrorists. They're just calling them 'the terrorists'." He continued on—he has an acute mind for numbers, distances, velocities and the like and was rattling off flight numbers, capacities and altitudes like another man might hockey stats.

When we hung up, I cheated and leaned to the right so the afternoon sun licked my face much earlier than nature's schedule.

The Terrorists. Them. Us. US of A. Tiny me.

That was one, one-thirty. Did I say that?

Now it's three. I am in the chair, the chair that will make gouges on the back of my legs that are more pronounced than cellulite. It doesn't matter; there is no mirror here to stand before and be judged. Actually, I have been sauntering around naked all day, trying to get comfortable with what is me.

The telephone rings again. It is old-fashioned and rings shrill and long. My heart skips a beat whenever it *brrrrrrings*. It is someone from Nanaimo, looking to deliver curtains to a Hornby Island B&B. Next island over, I say, still quaking from the ring.

Wrong target.

I've found myself scrambling to the phone, positioned just inside the door, though I don't know why. There is no answering machine to kick in. I am not playing hooky from work; there's no need to answer in a strangulated, flu-induced voice. I am here of my own volition. And verition.

Anyway, my own choice and my own truth.

I doze and stare all afternoon. At five o'clock, it rings again.

Goddamn it. Can I not answer?

After the eleventh ring, I snatch up the receiver and bark, "Hello."

"Hel-*loo-hoo*. I called to wish you Happy Anniversary." My aunt, Sara, calling from Red Deer. She frequently adds syllables to innocuous words. She's also one of the three people I'd given the number to in a moment of lucidity or stupidity. That, and she had called me just as I was packing and demanded a contact number. Her pause is long, but only because I haven't responded. "So, Happy Anniversary. Were you down at the beach?"

Just some of my lies rear up, surge like waves ready to break.

I had managed not to tell anyone that David, my husband, had moved in with his cousin. Especially not Sara, my only living relative, who would be personally wounded: she, after all, had introduced us a few lifetimes ago. Who am I kidding? She'd handle it. It's me, too scared to tell anyone that I drove David away. It's my fault.

No, I am simply here to paint the final pieces for a show in November, to finish painting the series of woman and her breakdown. The eighth, the last, is the woman in her own womb. Full circle. I don't plan to attend the Richards Street opening.

"Thanks. Thank you muchly," I answer with false heartiness, gripping the clunky receiver tightly. "And yes, I have taken the easel to the beach."

"What's Dave up to tonight? Has he phoned yet?"

I glance at the clock, though I know the approximate time. Such specifics were not to be necessary on this trip. "He'll call after six," I assure.

Assure whom?

"After six. Of course. We've got that . . ."

"Alberta/BC daytime deal," I finish.

"Yes. Twenty-three dollars. There's a cap on the minutes, but we never reach it."

"That's good," I say, gazing at the choppy, glistening water and thinking about how busy George Bush will be; about collecting oysters; what the guy at the store will wonder if I buy more wine today.

"Have you had the news on?" she gushes. A Cuisinart, perhaps a blender, is whirring in her background like a helicopter.

"No," I fudge my knowledge; no one knows about Abe. I do not ask, "Why?"

"The United States has been attacked by terrorists! The World Trade Center, the Towers . . ."

" . . . in New York," I append.

" . . . in New York," she echoes. "They've been bombed, well, airplanes deliberately ran into them and then the buildings imploded and there's something in the White House and something with a 'P'. P-p-p-p . . ." she struggles.

"Pittsburgh?" I offer.

"Pittsburgh!" she finishes triumphantly. She hasn't heard me.

I am silent. Still astonished, but in a faker way. "Holy cow," I finally say.

I don't want to know this, dammit!

"Who's claiming responsibility?" It has been, after all,

several hours since Abe's initial report. A lot can happen in a few hours.

"Eastern somethings," she says simply. "Maybe Afghanistan. The Palestinians. They're still just saying, 'the terrorists.' It's like Pearl Harbor."

"But it's not," I counter instinctively. "Right? I mean, you guys knew who bombed Pearl Harbor right off, right? And it was in the middle of a bona fide war."

I am getting myself all knotted up. I have to get off the phone. I silently curse her, and Abe, for destroying my four-day bubble with this knowledge. It is discombobulating because I know it's bigger than watercolour premieres, cousins, seductively curved dicks and inside-out wombs.

"Listen, I have to hit the outhouse," I say feebly. "Thanks for the good wishes."

"Okay!" she says cheerily. "I hope you create your Renwar!"

I know whom she means and shake off the harsh pronunciation of my mentor.

"Yes. Thanks, Auntie Sara. Okay, bye for now. Call any time." I hang up and nudge my paint supplies under a bunk with my toe. Out of sight, and all that. It only works for the tangible.

My Renoir. That was the ruse, perhaps even a potential side bonus to this solo sojourn, but not its basis. Right now, I don't even want to look at the thumbnail sketches of number eight, "Imploded Woman."

What is to be the self-portrait.

I pour a second, generous Hochtaler and squat on the front lawn.

Tens of thousands of people will be dead: agnostics, atheists, Jews, Christians, Muslims. Hindus. Buddhists. People that were possibly something spiritual at some time, but have long forgotten how they expressed it.

Now what?

The shadows are lengthening before my eyes. Why does the sun seem to set so fast? Faster than it moves across the sky all day, I mean. Like it's saying, Okay; I'm gonna go for it now. I'm finished with you people.

Going, going, gone.

Smash.

Inside, a little before nine, I am in the rocking chair, a nubbly, crocheted quilt wrapped around me. I had oysters for dinner, steamed in the microwave. I almost couldn't eat them; felt sorry for them that I was forcing them out of themselves. When I pierced them with my fork, their plump bodies collapsed and the salt water within them gushed freely. Much freer than blood.

I hear the wail of an air-raid siren from the base across the water in Comox and tense up—almost panic—except I don't have enough energy to take my feelings that far. What now? Then I remember, the cabin owner cautioned me that it goes off all the time, a training thing.

The phone again. Unpluggable.

"It's David," he says. Like I wouldn't know the voice.

"Hmmm."

"I didn't know if it was appropriate to phone and say Happy Anniversary or not." He pauses, waiting for my confirmation, but I have no idea either. "So, I decided I would. I hope that's okay. I'm not disturbing you?"

I am disturbed all right. My soul is disturbed, is being beaten around my body like a clamshell in a winter storm.

"Not at all. I was . . ." I am about to saying painting, or at least reading, but I am tired of pretense, for once. "I was just sitting."

"Well, I cheers'd us with a beer."

"Really? What did you cheers? The last month or the first twelve years?"

I have thrown him off course. He clears his throat. "All of it, in a way. I guess I was saluting the good times, in general."

"Ah," I say, suddenly unable to control my inexplicable irritation. "So, the first year and a half?"

He sighs. I click my tongue. This is better than lethargy, no?

"Listen! Have you had the news on?"

This again. This global disaster. "Yes. Sara phoned."

"My God! It's surreal. New York is covered in dust. It looks like snow. The looks on people's faces . . ."

"Has anyone claimed responsibility?" I ask again. Assigning blame has always been very important to me.

"Nah. Probably Afghanistan. All in the name of Allah."

I don't like this umbrella reasoning. "Allah?"

"That's what the guys'd've yelled before crashing the plane. 'In the name of Allah'."

"Yes, *he* did it in the name of religion, the peon, but that's not what it's about, is it? Anything so drastic must have hidden agendas." I think about my own. In the background, I hear Peter Jennings. "Turn up the tube."

"Jesus," he says, after we both listen for a moment. "It's

World Peace Day. Goddamn assholes, starting a world war on World Peace Day."

"Well, that clarifies the 'why today' question."

Total precision and planning. Unlike me, unlike my life schedule that ebbs like the tides. Why didn't I do it the first day? Why not yesterday? Will I at all?

I want escape, but not in that way anymore.

What now?

"Well, anyway . . ." I venture.

"Yes. Okay. Enjoy your time. Well, not enjoy. You know. Work hard."

"Uh-huh." Strange, how awkwardness and easy comfort can co-exist.

"Lissa? You're okay, right? Doing, feeling, okay?"

What to say? Yes, I am; a benevolent hand has reached into me and stirred the sandy bed of my plan, made its waters too murky to proceed. Or no, I'm not okay; I cannot pin down my soul. Come for me now, David? Say good-bye forever?

"I'm okay, David. Thanks."

"Okay. Call me when you get back to the city. We'll get together and . . ."

" . . . figure things out."

"Yes."

I will have things figured out, long before that.

I hang up and wrap myself up in the quilt again. It's almost dark. The light is grainy, like being underwater. I take out the orange tablets that Dr. Stanton prescribed. The ones I said I'd die before taking. He'd said, "You might very well. It's pills and voluntary counselling or the hospital, where everything you can imagine is mandatory. Take your pick. Take two a day, with food. No alcohol, it's counter-active. Make an appointment for when you get back."

I swallow them with the last of the wine. Baby steps to serenity.

I think about the peons, the hijackers that sacrificed themselves. In the name of Allah.

For what cause would I give myself?

Only myself. I have only ever thought about killing myself, to escape myself.

Selfish, wretched bitch, a voice says. You want to pin down your soul, you reach inside and find it, grasp it. Do whatever it takes to never let it go. The voice resonates in stereo from the shores, the boughs, down the flue of the chimney.

I want to learn if the sun rises as quickly as it sets.

ALAN TWIGG

Canada

I like the way nobody talks
On a Canadian bus.
I like the way nobody sits beside one another
Unless it's absolutely necessary.

We have so much space in Canada
We have learned to revere it.
We have so much silence in Canada
We have learned to revere it.

If you hurry out of the elevator first
I don't want to know you.

Some people say Canadians are too polite—
As if respect for space and silence are unnatural.
But geography is destiny.
Watch the other animals.
They huddle. They scheme. They gnarl.
We are the true north, wild and careful.
We stand on guard with our backs to the wind.

If it's true, as Pierre Berton likes to say,
A Canadian is someone
Who knows how to make love in a canoe,
There can't be many of us left.
What does a Canadian say after making love?

"Thank you. That was wonderful.
And I promise it won't happen again."

Tom Connors should be the Poet Laureate.
The capital should be at Portage & Main,
At the centre, not center.
But we are all up against America
So not evolving feels like progress.
Our most famous prime minister
Was famous for his shrug.
The Queen still visits.
Cree is still not an official language.
One of our provinces retains the adjective British
Even though roast beef is an ethnic dish
As Peter Newman liked to say
Before he went to live in Switzerland.

Our dreary national anthem is an embarrassment.
Nobody knows who wrote it.
We murmur along at hockey games
Gazing at the lyrics on the Jumbotron.
They snuck in "God keep our land"
In the same way we got Free Trade.
Nobody protested.
[In 1968 a special Joint Committee of the Senate and
House of Commons recommended some changes
in the Stanley Weir text. Bill C-36 was passed.
The French lyrics were unaltered.
The dirge-like melody was only officially proclaimed

the National Anthem on June 24th, 1980,
supposedly 100 years after it was first sung.]
And what does that line mean,
"In all thy sons command"?
Where are the daughters?
People would think you were nuts
If you took the words seriously.
Words and music together make art.
And we don't trust art.

Riding this bus along the 49th parallel
To where my Dad is dying,
I've been trying to remember all the lyrics
To "Canadian Railroad Trilogy,"
Wondering whether anyone wearing Walkmans
Has heard of Gordon Lightfoot.
"She said the man in the gabardine suit was a spy"
     will outlast
"Behind the blue Rockies the sun is reclining."
We accept this as inevitable. We are all second fiddlers
On the roof of the United States.
We're the dutiful daughter who didn't leave the Empire.
It was Robertson Davies who told me that.
He was wearing a black eye patch
And he didn't want to be photographed.
He called Brian Mulroney an arselicker
But I couldn't use it.
Even our best storyteller was reserved.
And before him, we had Hugh MacLennan.
Has anyone on this bus heard of Hugh MacLennan?

I saw the heroism etched in his face
That day in Montreal, wearing his beret,
With his heart on his sleeve
He was painfully son-hungry.
It doesn't surprise me
I should think of him now.
I don't see a lot of fathers on this bus.
I don't see a lot of leaders in this country.
A constant sense of smugness and foreboding binds us
Instead of the CPR and CBC.

I feel a sense of belonging in Canada
That is more about
Poetry & manners
Than pride & prejudice and patriotism.
I don't love this country.
It's not mine to love.
Another person is getting on the bus.
I hope they don't sit next to me.

CAROL MATTHEWS

Living in ASCII

Before I open my eyes I feel the nausea, a sinking weight at the core of my being. I go to my husband's study, hoping for comfort, but Stephen is in a fury and is loudly cursing the computer. He complains that he's just lost the first part of the paper he is writing for an English department meeting. The paper is about the stupidity of numerical grading practices, the impossibility of reducing everything to symbols.

"Those words are not really lost, Stephen, they're somewhere in cyberspace. You need to find a way to track them down in ASCII-land."

Stephen gives me a cool look and a raised eyebrow. Living in ASCII would suit him. A life like the inside of an essay. Immediate and impersonal. A life with form, but not necessarily with substance.

"How did you get home last night, Tannis? Did someone drive you?"

I try to collect my thoughts. Recollect my actions.

"More important, perhaps, where is your car?"

I wish he wouldn't make such a big deal out of avoiding

words that end in "ly." Stephen will never say "important-
ly" but he should, since he is actually asking the question in
an important manner. And surely how I got home is, in fact,
a more important question.

"The last thing I remember was singing "O Canada" out
in Adrienne's yard," I tell him. "Standing at the edge of the
ravine, arm in arm, singing our national anthem. Yvette
sang in French." Sometimes a small detail makes all the dif-
ference to Stephen, but not today. He is angry about the loss
of his words, the loss of the car. About who knows what
other losses.

⸱⸱

I try to piece together the events that led up to my home-
coming and might eventually lead me to my car. I remember
arriving at Adrienne's house. Apprehensive. Knowing how
important the evening was for Adrienne. Ever since Louise
moved in with her, Adrienne has been intent on bringing
groups of women together for social evenings.

When she asked me to the dinner party, I thought at first
that Adrienne meant me to bring Stephen, but she said no,
that she and Louise felt it was important to spend time in
the company of women.

"We've lost our ability to nurture ourselves as women
together," Adrienne had explained. "Louise says women
have to find a place where we can flourish alone, and only
then will we be ready to enjoy the company of men."

That's Louise talking. I try to get along with Louise, for
Adrienne's sake, but we just don't like each other. When

she talks to me she rocks back on her heels in a way that drives me crazy. She's a jock, and her ideas are stupid, but Adrienne adores her, so I say nothing.

The dinner was wonderful. A large, steaming bowl of African chicken stew, *doro wat*, which was decorated with blue and orange flowers, all edible and, as Louise noted, healthful. Plates heaped with fresh prawns, covered in finely chopped hot chilies and surrounded by sliced limes and sprigs of parsley. A soufflé of yams and coconut milk, and a salad of cucumbers and orange rinds. Garlic, ginger, roses, tinkling silver, and women's voices. Michaelmas daisies spilling from the large clay vases that Adrienne sculpts. In the sunroom at the end of the kitchen, enormous geraniums flowered alongside miniature persimmon and pomegranate trees. In the background, Bessie Smith belted out the blues.

Several women were from the university, and a couple from the hospital where Louise used to work. Louise had also invited Betsy, a staff person at her physiotherapy clinic, and Yvette, a Swiss student who was doing a locum at the clinic. Yvette's husband was killed in a skiing accident two years ago, and she came to Canada to escape painful memories. Casual, and elegant, in jeans and hiking boots, she wore a silk shirt that exactly matched her eyes.

"Would you call that colour aquamarine?" I asked. "Or is it teal?"

I am obsessed with the blues. The music and the colours. I announced that I had a list of twenty-six shades of blue and was always looking for more. The women around me took up the challenge cheerfully, as they sat at card tables covered with printed cloths and tiny bud vases of mint and nasturtiums. An attractive group of women, decked out in their exotic outfits, artistic jewelry, and gypsy colours, including a surprising number of shades of blue.

"Sapphire . . . azure . . . teal . . . periwinkle . . . cyan . . . cerulean," they called out.

"Light blue doesn't count as a colour. 'Kinda blue' doesn't either," I argued. "No, not *NYPD Blue.* You've still got eleven to go!"

The conversation was congenial, full of lively anecdotes about food and restaurants and kitchen misadventures intermingled with admiring comments about the dishes that were being set before them. Adrienne produced triumph after triumph. She wore a yellow and tangerine flowered sarong, and glowed, warm and round, like a golden sun.

I remember an argument that started with the crème brûlée and carried on right on through the *sambuca con mosca.* It was about a rape trial that had concluded the day before. Adrienne and Louise were members of the Sexual Abuse Victims' Emancipation group (SAVE), and they had attended the trial.

"I hate the confrontation between the victim and the defendant," Adrienne said. "I don't see why the victim has to have any contact with the man who raped her."

"Don't you think it needs to be brought out in the open?" Betsy asked. "How can anything be salvaged, if it isn't brought into a public forum and examined? Confrontation is unavoidable."

"I think you're wrong. I don't see why she has to be there at all, and certainly she should never have to look at that man again. The woman always loses in that encounter."

"What does she lose? The healing, the recovery, has to do with open and complete testimony about what happened. Acknowledgement. Public witness."

"Betsy's right," Louise said, and Adrienne slunk back into the kitchen. Louise and Betsy settled into a corner together, still talking about the trial. I remember thinking that Louise looked like a Weimaraner. Lean, well-built, swift. And mean, I thought, watching her move in on Betsy.

I know I played the guitar and we sang songs from the sixties. I remember Yvette's beautiful voice singing *Il y a longtemps que je t'aime, jamais je ne t'oublierai.* I have a clear picture of us standing at the edge of the ravine singing "O Canada" just as the sun was coming up. Betsy and Louise were not there and, although most of us were laughing, Adrienne was trembling. I realized it was from tears, and tried to comfort her. And after that, after that . . .

⸱⸜

Of course it's a slow process to recreate an evening, to drag reluctant memories from a sodden brain, and this information is not making Stephen any happier. We don't seem to have any milk, he observes, and he can't continue his work unless he has more coffee. If I had my car I would offer to go to the store, but I don't like to drive his vehicle.

"Go home, peckerheads!" he shouts at the cars that are lined up on the street outside. It's a busy street, but Stephen will not to say how much that bothers him, the house being his choice.

"The traffic is bad."

"It's not the traffic I'm talking about, Tannis," Stephen snaps. "I just want these peckerbrains to go home."

When he leaves, I go to the deck and gaze out to the mountains and the ocean, contemplating my hangover which I imagine as being a lot like living in ASCII. Living on the edge. Or beyond. In the abyss.

As it happens, Stephen should have just waited a few minutes longer, because Yvette appears at the door, returns the car, and fills me in on the rest of the evening. She didn't know what had happened between Adrienne and Louise, but she did know that when Nelson, Betsy's brother, had arrived to pick her up, both Betsy and Louise had disappeared.

"This was a lucky thing for me," Yvette says, laughing excitedly. "It was a wonderful night. Do you not like him, Tannis? Is he not attractive?"

Now I faintly remember a gentle, craggy sort of man helping me to my door. And, yes of course, he and Yvette drove me home last night and then borrowed my car.

"He is a biologist and he had been looking for someone with climbing experience to help him collect cormorant eggs for an experiment he is conducting, measuring the level of dioxin in the eggs. We went on an expedition together early this morning."

Nelson and Yvette had struck up a conversation as they waited for Betsy to return. Yvette doesn't drink at all, and she was probably the only person at the party who was capable of a sober conversation with a serious man like Nelson.

"They are an endangered species, you know, Tannis,"

Yvette explains, referring to the cormorants. "This is one of the few areas where they still flourish, and even here they are probably contaminated by the pollution from the pulp mills."

She can't tell me enough about her adventure. The eerie drive at dawn to Chemainus where, with Nelson's special permit, they were able to pass through a gas installation plant, through the fences, past the armed guards to reach the cliffs where the cormorants were nesting. Yvette says the place stank and in fact that Nelson identified it by the stench of the birds' poop. The problem was so severe that the trees were black and dying.

"Weren't you afraid?"

"Nelson was frightened," she laughs. "He is afraid of heights, but still he did it. You know? I showed him how to rappel. It took him five trips to do it, and he was terrified, actually, but he went down and got three eggs to bring back."

"Why didn't you let him hold the rope, Yvette?" I don't know anything about climbing, but I know that Yvette weighs a lot less than Nelson and she is an experienced climber.

"That's what he wanted," she admits. "But it was no good. I didn't trust him to be looking after me. I was the one who had the experience and knew how to hold the rope. He was scared, and you know, Tannis, when I saw him there, suspended over the edge, helpless and determined, he seemed like a symbol of courage. I think that's why I fell in love."

If we had more time I'd like to talk to Yvette about how the word *egg* is the origin for the word *edge*, and is also related to the word *eager*. I'd tell her about the symbolism of eggs, about the way the inside of the egg, in its darkness, contains the sunshine. Like the darkness before the dawn. But Yvette says she must leave. Now that she has found Nelson she doesn't want him to disappear.

My head is clear as I drive to Adrienne's house, and I realize, as I walk towards her door, that this is a house I always want to enter. The winding stone path is overhung with clematis and climbing yellow roses and dense with the scent of carnations and lavender. On each side of the doorway are large statues of vine maidens holding round bowls from which trail lobelia and nasturtiums.

Adrienne opens the door, her arms folded tightly over her indigo kimono, her eyes tragic and dark as pansies, the room behind her a shady glade. When we hug, I feel the warmth of her body under the cool silk of her robe. My pulse races at the sensation.

"Thank you," she says, "for taking care of me."

"Has Louise come back yet?"

"She phoned this morning and says she'll be here tonight. I'll wait."

"You deserve better." All the work she put into that party just to please Louise and make a good impression on Betsy. Peeling, chopping, blanching, sautéeing. Making perfect little individual crèmes brûlées. I notice that she has a bad burn on her left hand. How gentle she is, I think, how generous.

"Oh," she says, pressing her hand to her mouth. "Deserve."

"I can't stay. I just wanted to make sure you're all right."

"I'm all right," she says, and gives me another hug. "It's not as bad as you think."

When Stephen returns, he's in a good mood because he has bought a bag of hot red and yellow peppers, and also because he got to tell the produce man at the grocery store why he should not put quotation marks around the word *fresh*. He is sprightly and spirited, and suddenly I see him as he was when we first knew each other, a quarter of a century ago, in Vancouver. I remember we'd sat side by side on the lawn of a suite he had just rented on Point Grey Road, listening to a record of *The Four Seasons*. Next door, two brown monkeys were playing catch with a large orange.

"Not a thing out of place," he'd said, pointing at the carpet of green grass that led right to the edge of the cliff, the blue water, the white house, and the brown monkeys throwing the orange orange. Vivaldi playing all the while.

We are different people now. We look at the same ocean from the other side of the Strait. Our life together has come full circle and has a roundness that I want to preserve. For the moment, I've had enough of schisms, division, edges and losses, and I want to recover things, bring them back together. And yet, sometimes, when I let it all slip away, I seem to see through to what really matters. On a symbolic level, at least, where everything turns into pure sign.

If I were to tell the true story, I would write it not in words but in symbols, the way Stephen's paper on stupidity appeared in its final ASCII print-out. It would be very short and very true. It would go like this: moon, woman, woman; man, bird, sun; heart, heart, heart, heart, heart; rock, scissors, paper. The title would be *egg*. That would be the whole story.

JAN DEGRASS

Opening the Egg

It could not be Granny Yevtushkin beckoning at Moscow's Izmailovo Market this Saturday morning. Granny Y had just died in a Toronto hospital. I was certain of this fact because my father had phoned to let me know. By some miracle unprecedented in the Russian telephone system he had managed to place the call from his home in Toronto directly to my Moscow hotel room.

"Michael, she's gone," he said, always a man of few words. "She spoke fondly of you at the last."

The family had known, had seen her poised for death, following the stroke that was helped along by too many varenikies cooked in butter.

She died on Friday. I was stunned when she reappeared at the market on Saturday morning.

The resemblance was uncanny. This woman stood just like Granny Y, with firm, thick ankles planted in worn shoes. She wore a dark blue skirt stretched over her stomach and a kerchief tied under her chin. She caught my eye and pointed to the wooden eggs displayed at her feet. They were smooth, plain, turned, birch wood. Artists bought them, painted them with traditional designs and sold them to the tourists.

I moved closer and picked up a decorated one.

"One hundred rubles," she told me.

"No, please, I am not looking for eggs," I said in the style of Russian that Canadian kids learn from their immigrant grandmothers.

She shook her head. "You buy egg," she said in English. She even ordered me around like Granny Y. Most of the vendors of lacquer boxes, stacking dolls and Turkish-style rugs in this outdoor marketplace had at least enough English to help them trade with tourists or merchants like me who bought Russian handicrafts and art to peddle back home in Canada.

I studied the egg. It was similar in appearance to the hand-painted egg that sat in Granny Yevtushkin's kitchen for all the thirty years of my life. But this egg was solid wood while Granny Y's egg was hollow; it rattled teasingly when her children and later, her grandchildren, shook it. Though it had a hairline crack around its middle she would never let us open it, no matter how much we pleaded. She told me the egg contained the most important thing—the secret of life.

What would happen to Granny's egg now?

⁓

The funeral was held the day of my return from Russia. My sister Ellen picked me up at the Toronto airport. She was dressed in yards of crepe—a black dress and black felt hat with a veil such as Garbo wore fifty years ago.

"Let's go. We're late for the funeral," she said by way of greeting.

"I'm happy to see you too, Ellen. Yes, I had a good trip. Thanks for asking."

"Sorry . . ." she softened, wheeling the airport cart expertly out the door. "It's been stressful. The cousins are here from California. You know how Cousin Bernie can be. Why they can't stay with Hannah, I don't know. (Hannah is my other sister.) I've had Pete and his dog as well. (Pete is her ex.) Then I'm in charge of Granny Y's estate, you know, and we can't find her safety deposit box key—which means we can't find the will." She looked about ready to burst.

"Breathe, breathe," I reminded her.

"And then there's all this business about the egg."

I stopped dead on the busy pedestrian crosswalk. "The egg?" The image flashed again—that old babushka last Saturday. "You know I had the weirdest experience in the marketplace last week . . ."

But Ellen was already racing ahead to her illegally-parked sedan at the airport's main entrance. Snatching the ticket from the windshield, she unlocked the door and threw my bags in.

There was no more conversation until we pulled up at the Levin and Levin funeral parlour less than an hour later. The elder Levin stood at the door to greet us by our Russian names. "Lena, Lenochka, my dear. Misha, my good man." They say he could be relied upon to serve a slug of vodka to the bereaved in his office, but with the Orthodox priest arriving today he would be on his best behaviour. "The family is already in the chapel," he told us.

Granny Y's huge family stretched across four generations. Her eighty-four-year-old sister, Ilse, survived her. Her children were in attendance, as were my sisters and their kids. They were all seated when we entered. Dad stretched out his arm to me for a brief, uncharacteristic hug. Hannah the Good sat, ramrod straight, with her husband and three children in a pew opposite. She deigned to give me a pious glance. The casket was on display, but it was obvious that the gathering had been waiting with impatience for us to arrive, so there was no chance for me to view Granny's body. That was okay. We had already said our goodbyes in hospital before I had left for Moscow.

Afterwards, we all trooped downstairs to a lounge for sandwiches and pirozhki. Pete, Ellen's ex-husband, asked me about my buying trip to the "old country," as he called it. Pete was Scots-Irish and what he knew about Russia you could fit in a pot of borsch. His heart was good though. Granny Y had liked him. As we were talking, I overheard some sort of hideous family confabulation just beginning, as in the old days when my mother was alive.

Hannah was saying, "We will not do any such thing when her body is scarcely in the ground." The others, including her husband George, were frowning.

"I'm out of touch—what's the problem?" I asked.

It was Andy, Ellen's eight-year-old, who answered me. "We're going to open the egg!" he said delightedly. "It needs a magic word: Open, dude! Cowabunga. Right, Mom?"

Ellen glared at him and drew herself up to her full height. "As executrix"—she rolled the r's and x's in the word—"of Granny's estate, I think it's far more important for us to find the will right now and let the family know where we stand, than it is to expend all this energy on an egg."

"But you can't find the safety deposit key," reminded Pete.

Bernie, the California cousin, chimed in, "Maybe that's what's in the egg—the key."

"Maybe you're right," said an aunt. "It rattles, doesn't it?"

"No," said my father. "Mother had that egg back in the 1920s, long before she ever got a safety deposit box. The key couldn't be in there."

"How do you know she didn't open it without telling us?" I said. "And how do we know the will exists? Has anyone seen it?"

I turned to Ellen who looked about ready to spit. "She said it existed. She told me."

By this time most of the other relatives had gathered around. Mr. Levin was nodding his head and even the Orthodox priest was eavesdropping. Hannah, who always senses the moment to pontificate, seized this one.

"We must put away this talk until after Granny is laid to rest," she intoned. "Then we'll hold a family reunion in celebration of her life and this matter will be discussed."

"So, we'll have that at *your* house this time, Hannah, shall we?" asked Ellen tartly. "Then you can cook for fifty people." The talk deteriorated in this fashion. Weary and jet lagged, I wanted only to return to my bachelor apartment to sleep.

Two months passed and the day for the suggested family reunion rolled around. Hannah greeted me at the door. I had thought about bringing a girlfriend, but I figured there's nothing surer than a family party to deter a potential partner from ever wanting to see me again. So I had decided to give Aunt Ilse a ride, instead.

A party atmosphere filled the air. Ellen and Pete were there and all the kids. Some of Granny's friends from the seniors' centre had turned up and a few aunts and uncles as well. The California cousins had flown in just for the occasion. Bernie was bubbling over with excitement. The wooden egg had been given a place of honour on the dining room table.

Only Ellen looked gloomy and Dad looked tired. "Try the potato salad," was all he said.

Hannah and George moved smoothly around the room taking drink orders and reminding me of hosts at an elegant soirée—not a wake.

"Do you like these stuffed mushrooms?" Hannah was saying. "It's one of Granny's recipes. I thought it seemed appropriate."

As Hannah spoke, I saw Ellen sit up and a little of the dark cloud shifted from her face. Abruptly, she left the room.

"I am in confusion," said Aunt Ilse finally, in a loud voice. We all listened. She was usually blunt in her pronouncements. "Are we here to mourn my sister, to read will, or to open blessed egg . . . or all three?"

"We won't be reading the will because Ellen still hasn't found it," chipped in Pete.

Hannah looked smug but was silent for once.

"You bitch," cried a strangled voice from the kitchen. "You knew . . ." Ellen swooped back into the living room bearing a large fat cookbook in one hand and a will in the other.

"It was in the cookbook all along," she exclaimed, then turned to Hannah, "and you knew—all the while I was trying to get into the safety deposit—you knew it was there."

"No! No really," Hannah protested. "I only found it while I was stuffing the mushroom caps yesterday. You should have guessed. She kept all her important documents in among the recipes."

Dad put down his plate and moved closer. The others fell quiet.

"Now, now, no quarrelling!" said Cousin Bernie. "If the will is found, and we're all gathered here fortuitously, then let Ellen read it." He rubbed his hands together eagerly.

It was pretty much as expected. Most of the estate went to father as long as he was alive, with bequests to the aunts and cousins, and a modest sum to Hannah and Ellen "for their children." It was clause eight that was the real shocker: "And to my grandson, Michael, who appreciates fine Russian craft, I leave my wooden egg. May he never open it until he truly wants to learn the secret of life."

I was dumbfounded. Everyone turned to stare at me. I felt some response was expected to the question that hovered over the living room. "That's what she always told me," I said, "that the egg contained the secret of life."

"When I was seven," said Ellen, "she told me that it contained my two front teeth."

"She told me that it contained a fabulously expensive Fabergé egg once owned by the Romanovs," said Hannah. "I didn't know she was going to leave it to . . . you."

Dad snorted. "She used to tell me that it rattled like birch trees at her old home on Katyushin Lake."

"We always heard that it was a pair of lucky dice for the day she would go to Las Vegas," said Cousin Bernie. "Looks like she told everyone what they wanted to hear."

Someone chuckled; I could have sworn it was ghostly laughter.

"Did she tell you what was in the egg, sweetie?" Ellen asked Andy.

He shook his head but his grin flashed yes.

"That's nonsense," said Aunt Ilse. "She was given that egg in 1920 by a Russian peasant who exchanged it for some food. What would he have with dice? Or Fabergé eggs?"

I shifted in my seat which had suddenly become the proverbial rock or a hard place. I began calculating odds that I would not get out of the room alive if I didn't open the egg in front of everyone. I remembered what the old babushka in the marketplace had said. "You buy egg." Darn right.

I cleared my throat. All eyes were upon me.

"Well," demanded Ellen, "are you going to open it?"

"Uh, of course." I went down without a whimper. Call it dishonour to Granny Y's memory, if you like. Or call it a genuine desire at age thirty to learn the secret of life. Only my Dad looked disappointed. He returned to his armchair.

"I even know how to open it," I went on. "The shop-keepers in the souvenir stores open them for tourists. They put the egg on the ground, like so, and roll it under one foot, like so. That usually loosens it."

I lifted the egg. My method had produced only a fine shade of difference in the hairline around the egg's middle. "I think this one has been varnished shut," I said. "We'll need a razor blade to slice around the crack."

"So that proves it's never been opened before," said Bernie, grabbing the egg and studying it.

"Not unless Granny Y re-varnished it afterwards," I replied.

George returned with a razor knife.

With the knife in one hand and the egg in the other, I hesitated. The group's will was palpable. At these moments—ironically, moments of greatest selfishness—we were as one, a complete, functional family unit. It was almost worth the stress.

Ellen had grabbed young Andy and held him in front of her. He stood two feet from my chin, eyes like saucers. They captured my attention. Once more I saw the image, the old woman in the marketplace—or Granny Y—set deep in the genes of his eight-year-old face. "Buy a trinket for your grandchildren," she had said. No, not a trinket. The Russian word was better translated as keepsake. Something you keep for your grandchildren.

I set down the knife. I rubbed that smoothly-turned birch wood from the forests of Russia against my sleeve, and I searched Andy's face—the Slavic eyes, the glistening cheeks like butter dumplings. He stared back.

"You don't have to open it if you don't want to," he said suddenly, looking wise. "I don't care."

"Someday I'll give it to you," I told him. He nodded. I put the egg into my pocket, excused myself politely and slid through the crowd.

"But what if it's really valuable? . . ." Hannah called out.

The door gave a satisfying slam behind me.

·⤳

Ellen wouldn't speak to me for many weeks afterward. Hannah was frosty. Aunt Ilse was pissed off because she had been left without a ride home from the party. Dad was his usual self. Pete decided to study Russian at night school in honour of Andy's new legacy. And Bernie flew back to California where he is reportedly still dining out on the story of the mysterious family egg.

DAN NEIL

Grace

I wait for my eggnog latte beneath red lights that hang like hot dripping strawberries and notice her at the counter. She is neat in tweed and angel hair and stockings thick enough to rebuff a cheeky winter. She pokes through her change purse with a thin white finger while she chats with a young girl who looks down at the coins as if she were entertaining some ancient spectacle. The clink of something forgotten. Quarters stacked like pancakes. Dimes and nickels in pairs. Pennies alone in impoverished segregation. My own mother did this very same thing. The totem of a generation.

There is a man looking over her shoulder. He is dressed for business. He holds a cellular phone in one hand and a leather bound organizer in the other. He tilts his wrist and glances at his watch. His feet shuffle. The dance of discontent. He peers intently as if doing so will bring about a swift transaction. But the old woman has no mind for his urgency and affirms each coin before the girl to ensure her that she has counted correctly.

Then the woman turns slightly and seems to feel the presence of the man's impatience. Perhaps it his restlessness that leans over her, or the weight of a world that she will never understand. The line grows longer. Still she counts and chats. He sighs with a dramatic out-breath and she turns to him fully and catches the churlish roll of his eyes.

I can see her hurt, the unjust wound washing over her. But the fine lines of her age do not flush. Her soft dark eyes gather, composed and certain. She does not yield to the temptation to be offended. She looks up to the man as if she stands at some threshold, a moment that bends before her.

"What are you having?" she says. Raspy and sweet.

The man stares down at the old woman as if unsure what was asked. There is a pause among the tables, talk momentarily stilled by something greater manifesting. Like them, I am compelled to be an observer, consider the distance between them. The outcome. What will he do?

Then he answers brusquely. "A tall dark. To go." He shrugs to demonstrate some rare humility.

"I will have one of those too," the woman says to the young girl. Change is counted one by one. She is unaware of compartmentalized time. The urgency of schedules.

At last she is done and sits with her tea at a table near to me. The man takes his coffee and thanks her. She does not hear. He looks uncertain, confused and stalled, his sour heart sweetened by kindness. He adds his cream and sugar. Stirs. He watches her. Her half smile. Then he steps to the door, answering to the incessant hum of striving and strain, but stops and turns back. I watch without looking. Afraid to disrupt the unravelling of a soul.

He moves towards her, his feet sliding across the tile floor as if caught in the pull of timelessness. She looks up to him as if she were waiting for a son. There is nowhere to go, nothing demanded. Patience has been recovered, the reunion of virtue, the touching of the great mystery.

"Do not mind me," she says softly like a child, "there are days when the girls behind the counter are the only ones I have to speak to."

"No, I forget," the man says. "I forget to stop and notice things."

"I suppose you are a very busy man," the woman says. "It is hard to find the time."

"It's that time of year. The rush and all that."

"I am in no rush," she says. She smiles.

"Yeah." He laughs then glances to us all encroaching. But he doesn't seem to mind. "That is all I have," she says. "Counting change. Sipping tea. Chatting to the young girls."

His eyes blink to fend off what appears to be tears. I don't believe it. Tough guy. She's got him. Nailed him to the cross of strivers.

"Thanks for the coffee," he says with his head lowered. He backs away. Self-conscious now.

"Thank you for coming, Tommy."

He stops and his eyes narrow. A swift frown of confusion. He turns away.

And as he leaves I notice the others watching. Their eyes never left the pair of them. One middle-aged woman removes a tissue from her purse and dabs the corners of her eyes. The end of some maudlin play. But there are smiles and an energy that I've never felt before, a sense of good. Hope and possibilities. The old peak experience. My throat closes and my chin crumples. Me too.

"That was very thoughtful of you," I say to her. I feel the need to be a part of her charity.

"It was my treat," she says leaning back to look up at me. As if I have suddenly materialized.

"You know him, then?" I say casually as I turn to take up my drink from the young girl.

"Why of course. That was my son Tommy."

I feel my jaw fall slack. I turn to the others still elevated in bliss. They are somewhere else. But I am here, uncertain now of her kindness, perplexed by the mingling of a grand lesson with a muddled moment. Something else. I don't know. There is only the old woman and myself caught in the tension of ambiguity. And the door. I could leave like the man, reclaimed and razed in a breath. Suck the nutmeg foam from my latte and leave. But I cannot move. She is different, brushed with the pallor of dementia. Robbed of grace. I feel her old eyes upon me. Dimmed it seems.

"I have said something wrong," she says. "I have upset you."

"No," I say. I don't look at her. I feel uncomfortable and want to dismiss her before she slips again. I am hot with shame, some truth she has revealed.

"I am sorry," she says. A sigh. "It has happened before. More so lately. So many feelings this time of year."

"No, don't be," I manage.

"My son Tommy died just before Christmas. A bad snowstorm in 1989."

"And that man, he reminded you of him?" Such treach-
ery of the brain. Who cares for this old woman?

"That was my Tommy. He is my son."

Then she reaches out to me and cups my hand in her
cold pleated palms. Hands that have cradled the world.
Hands that have held a son.

"Tommy seems like a good man," I say without knowing
why. It just comes out.

She smiles, patting the back of my hand. She trembles,
struggling with her frailty, drifting in and out like poor recep-
tion. Even the fleck of light in her eyes has left her. I can read
her torment like a long story that will not end happily.

"Yes," she says.

"Tell me about him," I say, sitting down across from her.

LES DESFOSSES

Lares

The nurse draws the curtain around the bed and leaves me alone with my mother, with her long, whistling inbreath and longer, sighing outbreath. Her mouth, shapeless without her dentures, sags open and I use a tissue to dab her chin and wipe the saliva from her lips.

"Even in a deep coma she can still hear you," the nurse told me.

I don't believe it. I don't believe she hears anything, but I lean close, my mouth to her ear.

"It's okay, Mom. I'm right here beside you. Everything is going to be all right."

As, after my prayers, she used to whisper, "Good night darling. I'll see you in the morning," leaving me safe and warm, clutching my teddy bear to my chest, hearing her soft footsteps receding and the gentle closing of the door.

⁓

The CT scan showed a huge white blot of blood against the darker background of the brain. "I'm afraid there's no way she can survive such a massive bleed." A young doctor, blond and bearded, watching me to see how I was taking it. "I can call a neurologist for a second opinion if you like."

"No. That won't be necessary."

"We'll keep her comfortable."

"That's all I expect."

While they move her to the third floor, I go to the pay phone outside the gift shop. Gloria won't be home yet—this is one of her volunteer days—so my only call is to my sister in Calgary. She asks a few questions, promises to be here tomorrow morning and tells me that this was the will of God. No doubt it will also be the will of God that we stage the full religious ceremony—hymns and prayers and a sermon promising a better place. I suppose it's appropriate. My mother never lost her child-like faith, or ever doubted that my father was up there somewhere, like a new star in the night sky, looking down on us.

She'd quote Proverbs: "Trust in the Lord with all thine heart; and lean not unto thine own understanding." Once, when I'd heard that verse once too often, I told her it was meaningless; we know nothing of the Lord, or anything else, except through our own understanding. Which was as close as we came to discussing religion. I saw no reason to tell her I was neither a Christian nor an atheist nor an agnostic because, so far as I was concerned, the whole God question was nonsense.

The third-floor nurse is thin and fortyish, steel-rimmed glasses and steel-grey hair. "Right this way," into the ward, opening the curtain and crossing the room for a chair. I take the chair from her hands and carry it to my mother's bedside.

"It happened very quickly," she says. "Your mother didn't suffer."

"I know."

"It could have been a lot worse."

"I know that, too."

Once every week for three years, we visited my mother's older sister in the nursing home, bracing ourselves against the smell of old bodies and the pleading cries of wild-eyed women in wheelchairs: "Won't somebody please take me home?" We spent an hour in the visitor's lounge, beneath the brightly coloured, large-print posters, my mother chattering away, my aunt's mind meandering, sometimes with us in that stuffy room, sometimes back in high school in 1920s Winnipeg. The day I put down the phone and told my mother her sister was dead, she didn't even look up from the TV.

"She's better off," she said.

⸺

A telephone rings, soft-soled footsteps come and go, the woman in the next bed moans and a young nurse offers cheerful encouragement. My mother's breathing seems a little slower, but I'm not sure. The doctor said she could live as much as twenty-four hours. Twenty-four hours ago she

was in her own living room, surrounded by her junky fig-
urines, leaning forward, an arm's length from the TV,
watching some soap opera or cooking show.

The nurse parts the curtain. "Are you all right?"

"I'm fine."

"How is she doing?" She steps in and leans over the bed.
"Her breathing is slower." The nurse studies me and says,
"I'll check back in a while."

"I'll be okay."

.‿

The house will have to be sold. Walls and floors scrubbed. The
ancient dining-room drapes, the plastic bathroom curtains
and the broken tape-deck will go to the dump. All her dusty
doodads and tacky artifacts to garage sales and second-hand
stores. My sister will get the jewelry. I'll keep a few things,
some living-room furniture, her 27-inch TV, but not her TV
lamp. That god-awful ceramic duck—I can't wait to see the
last of that thing.

.‿

I once suggested my mother sell her house and move to a
retirement apartment, but she wouldn't hear of it.

"This is my home," she said. "I've lived here forty-three
years and the only way I'm leaving is feet first."

I was retired and divorced so it didn't matter where I
lived. I built a suite in her basement, moved in and did the
maintenance and house cleaning and took her shopping. I,

later Gloria and I, took her out to a movie and dinner every week.

"Any movie you'd like to see, Mom?"

"Any movie you kids pick is okay with me."

Sometimes, for her, we went to movies like *Aladdin* or *Beauty and the Beast*. We also took her to serious movies, but it was hard for her to see the screen and harder to follow the story. "Well, that was quite a picture," she'd say as we left the theatre, waiting to hear what we thought.

"Where would you like to eat, Mom?"

"Any restaurant you kids like is okay with me."

She insisted on picking up the tab for every second dinner, though it always included a bottle of wine she hadn't shared. No, it was never a demanding job, caring for my mother. I did wonder, sometimes, when I'd be free to travel again.

⁓

An hour passes within the white curtain, beside the white bed and my white-haired mother. Two hours. Three hours. Gloria will be home now and I should call. My mother's breathing has slowed to a laboured sucking and wheezing. My mother, who was never silent, is slipping into silence. My mother, who never met a stranger. Who struck up conversations with other shoppers in supermarkets, with other diners in restaurants, with other travelers on planes and ferries. My mother, loud and clear in a crowded waiting room, when she heard them paging Doctor Porter: "Doctor Porter! That's the doctor who operated on my hemorrhoids."

⁓

"I know you sacrifice a lot for me," she said, a few weeks ago, and I wish I'd said it wasn't a sacrifice. "You'll be a rich man when I die," showing me her broker's statement, and I wish I'd said I hoped that wouldn't be any time soon. I don't remember what I said, but I remember my calculations. Half of eight hundred thousand plus half of the house minus taxes plus my own money came to nearly a million dollars. A townhouse for two hundred thousand, invest the balance at, say, eight percent, and I'd have plenty to live comfortably and travel as much as I wanted. When she died. Which might not be for another ten years.

⁓

My mother gasps, shudders, relaxes and seems to sigh. And she is dead.

"Mom?" Pointless, but I put my mouth to her ear. "Mom?" Maybe I should call the nurse; the curtain parts and the nurse steps in.

"How is she? Oh . . . I see. She's gone." I expect her to draw the sheet over my mother's face. Instead, she asks, "Would you like to sit with your mother for a while?"

"Okay. I mean, yes, I would."

"Most people find it comforting to sit with their loved ones. It's a way of saying good-bye and fixing her in your memory."

The nurse leaves, I brush a stray hair from my mother's forehead and gently lift her jaw to close her mouth. When

I remove my hand, her mouth drops open. "Poor mom," I whisper. "Poor mom." Her face is already losing the last, faint traces of colour. How long should I sit here? How long does the average son sit with his dead mother? Would the nurse think me heartless if I left now?

Suddenly, it's time. I stand, kiss her forehead, whisper, "Good-bye Mom," step through the curtain and walk to the nurses' station.

"What should I do about the body?"

"Don't worry about that today," the nurse tells me. "You can call us tomorrow and you can come by and pick up her things from Security."

Maybe I ought to get it over with, but it's easier to do what the nurse suggests. "Okay. I'll call tomorrow."

I take the elevator to the lobby and the long hallway to the front door, overtaking a shuffling old man in a blue dressing gown with a rack and a hanging, intravenous bag, a pack of cigarettes in his skinny hand. Half a dozen people wait in the lobby, idly thumbing magazines or staring into space, smelling their own mortality.

·－

The glass doors slide open and I walk out into fresh air and the yellow-tinted sunlight of late afternoon. A bit cool, winter's on its way, but not just yet. It's been a fine September. My mother has been out in the yard every day, puttering, watering the flowers she keeps—kept—in her motley collection of pots and cans and plastic containers. I wonder if any of her plants are worth saving.

Seven-fifteen as I leave the parking lot. I could go to Gloria's, or call Gloria, but I drive to my mother's house and walk through the disorder of my mother's kitchen into the unfamiliar silence of my mother's living room. My mother's things wait, diffidently, like embarrassing relatives you don't quite know what to do with. Her dust-covered collection of kitsch. My ex-wife once referred to these things as *lares*, then had to explain that lares were Roman gods of households and ancestors. My Presbyterian mother was not amused to hear her treasures compared to pagan idols.

From the middle of the room, I scan the smiling elves on toadstools, the adorable children with umbrellas, the innocent shepherdesses and graceful ballerinas, the pottery deer and glass swans. I step to the piano and lift my parents' wedding picture from among the family photographs. My father, tall and dark, wears a black, double-breasted suit and a white boutonniere and stands behind my mother, holding her protectively against him. My mother smiles and leans back against her new husband. She wears white gloves, a 1930s white hat and a tight-fitting, white dress that reveals a barely perceptible tummy bulge. My first portrait. Which no one ever mentioned.

I put back the photo, cross the room and pick up the ceramic duck—a mallard drake, unnaturally bright, taking off from green and yellow ceramic reeds. It's unplugged, as is the TV, because my mother worried a plugged-in TV might start a fire. I told her that was impossible. I explained in detail why that was impossible.

"Yes, Jerry-pet. I'm sure you understand these things a

lot better than I do," and kept unplugging the television every night before she went to bed.

I carry the duck to the chesterfield and sit down, holding it in my lap, hefting it, turning it, examining the dusty light bulb and the C-shaped flowerpot. "Lane & Co. LA California 1954" inscribed on the bottom. I vaguely remember my parents taking a trip to California in the mid-fifties. She must have bought this duck as a souvenir. Taste? Forget it! But, didn't she love these things! Every one of them.

My mother at the kitchen table with a tube of glue, repairing the delicate leg of a tiny deer my father had knocked over when he was drunk. "There, there, you'll be just fine now." Did she always talk to these things? Or only after my father started spending a lot of time working out of town? "You'll look nice up here." "Don't you worry. Nobody is going to touch you." And something else. Something fluttering around the edges of my memory. Coming home from junior high, entering the basement—a rec room then, where my suite is now—and hearing my mother upstairs, slamming cupboard doors. "Does he think I'm blind? I'm supposed to wash his God-damned lipsticked shirts and keep my mouth shut?" I tiptoed out and went around to the upper door. "Hi Mom, I'm home."

"Hi darling. Your cookies and milk are ready." She sat with me at the kitchen table and asked about my day the way she always did. My sister came home from elementary school, my father from work, we had dinner and talked and laughed the way we always did. I thought it had been my imagination until I took out the garbage and saw a piece of white cloth among the tin cans and potato peelings. And more pieces stuffed in the bottom of the bag. As though an entire dress shirt had been chopped to shreds by pinking shears.

·ᵔ·

I lie back and balance the duck on my chest. He's frozen in the take-off mode, ceramic wings that can't beat, trapped forever in his ceramic swamp. Gloria has been divorced for ten years and tells me she's tired of living alone, but I couldn't leave my mother and it didn't seem right to make plans that depended on my mother's death. We have talked about travel. There are still a lot of places I want to see, but three weeks away from home and that is about as much as Gloria can imagine.

I sleep and dream of the duck. His beating wings, strong and confident, lift him high among towers of snow-white cloud. My mother sits on his back, waving down at me and smiling, blowing me a kiss. I wake up, cold and disoriented, cuddling the ceramic duck to my chest. It's dark outside, one in the morning, another day, a day since my mother died. Beyond the door, her departing footsteps already faded out of hearing.

I put the duck back where I got it and pick up the beige cardigan my mother left draped over the back of her TV chair. The wool to my face, the smell of her, comfort, dust and lavender, I step onto the patio and look up at the night sky. The Dipper is low to the northern horizon and Cassiopeia almost directly overhead. *Oh, Mom! Mom! Things I could have said. Or couldn't have said.* A single star moves from east to west, making its way among the constellations, but it's not one of those stars the poets write about. This one is man-made, a piece of space junk, tumbling and tumbling, from nowhere to nowhere.

PATRICK KING

The Birthday Wish

I never paid much attention to the old. They were nothing more than a race of aliens cohabiting my young world. So far distanced from me that I relegated them to the sidelines, worthy only of a curious glance. Tomorrow I will be 100. It is the young who are aliens now, and they are all I think about.

Youth is a skin shed, a cocoon, a past life. It is my paradise lost.

There are times I believe this is all a dream, and I'll wake up the twenty-five-year-old girl I am. But morning arrives and I am still in the nightmare. The aches have not thawed from my bones. My veins like swollen purple rivers continue to course through my hands. More liver spots, the brown crop circles that they are, have appeared.

I stopped looking at my reflection and having my picture taken when I turned sixty. Why would I want to discover another wrinkle amongst the thousand already creasing my face, to see my chin sag another two inches? Mirrors and cameras, like everything else in this world, are for the young.

The employees at the nursing home here tell me God has blessed me with long life. I shrug and laugh. He has cursed me and will them too, if they reach my age. Life is not sweet for a hundred-year-old woman. Mine revolves around strangers who take care of me. I have buried a husband and three children. All my friends are dead except Emily Martin who suffers from Alzheimer's in a hospital somewhere in New Brunswick. I do not have control over my bowels. My breasts are deflated dumbbells. I have a plastic hip and am forced to use a walker. I cannot bathe myself. I share a room with another old woman who because of a stroke has her mouth paralyzed open and cannot speak.

I am a relic. An unwilling artifact. I carry around memories like overstuffed suitcases.

My doctor, fool that he is, trumpets me as proof that a life span of a hundred years is possible. Mr. St. Claire, director of the Golden Oaks Home and an imbecile, has hovered around my bedside for the last two weeks. "You are the first person to reach a century at the home," he tells me with each visit. He gloats like a father whose child is the first to attend college in a family of rednecks.

He has ordered around-the-clock care for me. Not for my sake but his. I am the feather in his cap, the golden goose who will lay the hundred-pound egg. Tonight, Nurse Flight is on shift. She sleeps in the chair in the corner with an empty box of chocolates on her lap. Of all the nurses at the home, she is the worst. She prefers stuffing her mouth with sweets over tending to the needs of an old woman. She never runs the water past lukewarm when it is her turn to bathe me. Her rough hands never dry me off completely.

Her cold blue eyes do not hide the repulsion at having to clean me after I have soiled myself.

I listen to her snore and pray to God to let me die tonight. Let Nurse Flight have to explain to Mr. St. Claire that I died on her watch.

              ·⤳

I open my eyes and see Nurse Flight peering down at me. She grunts and nods. I do not merit a "good morning" or a "happy birthday." She collects her purse from the chair, inspects the empty box of chocolates, and tosses it in the garbage before leaving. God, as usual, has not answered my prayer. He has let me live another day. I have reached the age most aspire to but few attain.

Nurse Carim bounces into the room.

"Happy birthday," she says. She is the only staff member I like. She does not treat me like a child, or a vegetable. I envy her fresh flesh and enthusiasm. She reminds me of what I once was.

She hands me a box wrapped in pink paper tied with gold ribbons. I thank her and try to appear appreciative. Her quick skilful fingers help my arthritic ones unwrap the present. It is either soap or talcum powder, the perennial gifts for the old.

It is a bottle of gin. Liquor is outlawed at the home, and I am touched that she has put her job on the line for me.

"I figured that if you make it to a hundred, you're entitled to a drink or two," she says.

Mr. St. Claire flutters in like a deranged moth. Nurse

Carim shoves the bottle under my blankets and winks.

"Good morning, birthday girl," Mr. St. Claire cries and hands me a card. It has a picture of a tree in full autumn bloom and a bible carved in its trunk. "May God Bless You on Your 100th Year" is scripted at the base. The inside reads like a prayer, not a birthday verse. Why do the young think old people are close to God or even want to be?

Like a magician, he pulls an envelope from his suit pocket. He sits on my bed, dangerously close to the bottle of gin.

"This," he says, "is birthday wishes from the Queen." He waves the letter under my nose and holds it out like a bone to a dog, but does not let me take it. He pats my head, clears his throat, and reads aloud.

Did the Queen spout such diatribe when her mother hit one hundred, I wonder?

"I'm going to laminate and put it up in the front office," he says as if he has just ejaculated. He refolds the letter, stuffs it back into the envelope and returns it to his pocket. "I've got a big celebration planned for you this evening. Isn't that right Nurse Carim?"

She nods.

"We're going to have a birthday dinner, a cake and a bingo for entertainment. And I've made it mandatory that all staff and residents attend. I've invited the *Gazette* to take your picture and I've written a little notice to go under it."

Even worse than turning a hundred is having strangers all over the city gawking at my picture in tomorrow's paper.

"I don't want my picture taken, and I don't want a party."

Mr. St. Claire smiles and shakes his head.

"Now, now," he says. "Don't be cranky on your birth-day." He recites the line from a '70s poster about today being the first day of the rest of my life.

What bullshit. Whoever wrote that should have been shot, or at the very least be 110 now and confined to an oxy-gen tent in a ten by twelve room with no windows.

"Maybe we shouldn't, if Mrs. Roberts doesn't want it," Nurse Carim says.

"Nonsense," Mr. St. Claire replies. "It's all been arranged."

⁕

Nurse Flight stands beside me with the walker and demands I take hold of it.

"It's time for your birthday dinner," she says. "Everybody's gone to a lot of work for you, now get up."

I refuse.

She pulls me out of the bed and pushes the steel con-traption into my hands. I have drunk half the bottle of gin and stumble. Nurse Flight catches me before I fall. She sniffs around my mouth.

"You've been drinking!"

She flips my pillows over and rips the blankets from the bed while still holding on to me. She finds the bottle.

"Who gave you this?"

"None of your business."

One of the male staff pokes his head into the room.

"Everybody's waiting," he says. "Mr. St. Claire wants her out there."

"I don't have time to deal with this now," Nurse Flight says to me. "But you can be damn sure I will tomorrow."

"I'm not going," I tell her.

"Oh yes you are."

She throws me on the bed, rushes out and returns with a wheelchair. She plops me into it and pushes me out to the dining room. It is decorated like a child's birthday party at the local McDonald's. I am wheeled up to the head table with the Golden Oaks staff and placed beside Mr. St. Claire. I stare out at the yellow withered faces at the tables before me. Most of them are senile, and those who are not, do not know who I am. I spot my roommate, propped up in the back like a wilting sunflower. I am at a wake, not a birthday party.

Mr. St. Claire rises and stands behind me. He rests his hands on my shoulders and the pressure hurts. The gin rumbles in my stomach. I try to keep my eyes open because when I close them, my head spins.

"I introduce Mrs. Doreen Roberts, Golden Oaks' first centenarian," Mr. St. Claire announces and claps. His staff like seals join in. Nothing can save me from this indignity, and I am resigned to sit here like a decrepit puppet.

Mr. St. Claire speaks more gibberish. He talks more about me than to me. He rereads the letter from the Queen. And then the meal is served. Tough roast beef, dry mashed potatoes, bland carrots and warm cranberry juice. I eat very little.

After dinner, Mr. St. Claire clinks his glass of cranberry juice with a fork and toasts me. He beckons the apathetic, tall middle-aged man with the camera at one of the tables to come forward.

"This is Mr. Peevers from the *Gazette*," he says. "He's going to take your picture and make you famous."

Mr. Peevers extends his hand but I do not take it. Like many of the characters in Dickens' novels Mr. Peevers' name is symbolic of his nature. I am sure he is a pervert and would rather take pictures of young girls' underpants than of an old woman's jowls.

"Mrs. Roberts, tell us the secret to long life?" he asks and smirks.

I am drunk. I am a hundred years old. I can say what I want. I do not have to watch my P's and Q's. That is for the young.

"A good fuck," I say.

Mr. St. Claire blushes.

"How disgusting," Nurse Flight says. Many of the staff groan in agreement. I have committed the unforgivable. I have mentioned the subject the young think taboo for the old. Nurse Carim smiles over at me and I wink back.

Mr. St. Claire twirls his index finger beside his temple. "Probably going batty," he chuckles to Mr. Peevers. "At that age what can you expect?"

Mr. Peevers appears untroubled. I have captured his attention and he moves closer to frame his picture. The cake is wheeled in, aflame with a forest of candles.

"Take the picture when she blows out the candles," Mr. St. Claire instructs Mr. Peevers.

"Make a wish and blow," Mr. St. Claire says to me. "And don't tell us what it is or it won't come true."

What is a woman my age going to wish for? Another year? To have regular bowel movements? To feel soft green grass under my feet, not the hard linoleum of this prison? To be young again?

I wish for the evening to be as humiliating for Mr. St. Claire as it has been for me.

A stream of diarrhea soils my underwear. The stink infiltrates the room. Mr. St. Claire flinches. Mr. Peevers steps back. The cake is positioned before me. The writing on it is blurred. I cannot read it nor do I care what it says.

"Blow," Mr. St. Claire says.

The gin bubbles up my throat and I throw up over the lit cake.

Flash!

My head falls forward and Mr. St. Claire pulls it back before it hits the cake.

I vomit again. This time on Mr. St. Claire.

Flash!

I'm going to enjoy tomorrow's edition of the *Gazette*.

LINDA LEE CROSFIELD

Excess

Pegi's mother sent us care packages of homemade pasta—lasagna, fettucine, gnocchi—and ready-to-bake muffin mix which tasted just fine wrapped in cannelloni, raw and sweet and served alongside a heap of Minute Rice cooked in Grape Crush instead of water, followed by dessert, chocolate syrup drizzled on the tongue, the whipped cream chaser shot into the mouth from the aerosol can. The day we realized it wasn't cake we craved, but topping, we baked no more, mixing bowl after bowl of luscious butter icing which we much preferred to caviar, petits fours, canapés, meringues, hors d'oeuvres. And then there were the restaurants: L'Altro Mondo, where we'd get the most exquisite zabaglione with its egg yolks and Marsala wine whipped to a frenzy then poured down our throats; Yamase, the beef, sliver thin, you cooked in a boiling broth, sashimi, sushi and tempura so light that once a piece of carrot escaped the serving dish and floated halfway to the ceiling before someone caught it; The Seafood Place, where four and twenty fat and slippery oysters glistened on the half shell, four and twenty gritty, spicy oysters washed down with Dom Perignon and later cappuccinos, lattes, espressos, B-52's, flaming sambucas, followed by the best brandy, VSOP, and sometimes LSD. And in the summer there was nothing we wouldn't put on the barbecue except for steak tartare. Once, when Doug came in with a peanut butter sandwich, we tore it from his hands, leaving only the bit still clutched between his thumb and finger and afterwards he said he understood why it is the lioness who hunts for food. Next time we get together, after we catch up on each others' news of kids and husbands, cats and dogs, who's birthed, who's died, the awful state the country's in, we'll put on elastic-waisted skirts and comfortable shoes and head downtown where we'll reinvent the meaning of let's do lunch.

TOM WAYMAN

The Stone

The boss advances toward me across the room.
Before I can focus on his intent
he slams a huge stone into my stomach
and grinds it in.
I can scarcely breathe.
Through my pain and its weight,
he speaks.
But as I try to inhale, exhale,
instead of hearing anything I watch a silvery fluid,
viscous and lumpy,
waterfall over his lower lip
and shower onto the stone,
soaking my shirt and trousers
around the rock being jammed into my abdomen.

Then the boss has vanished
but the boulder
remains embedded. I feel a tug on each arm
and two colleagues propel me forward.
I stumble step after step,
half-bent over the mass of rock.
They lead me down familiar hallways
to the main entrance.
My guides, too, are talking
yet in my dizziness their utterances

appear a diluted version
of the words the boss said, the liquid this time
splattering over the corridor's linoleum
and across their shoes and mine.

I lean against the railing of
the front stairs outside, alone.
The acres of parked vehicles
wink and glisten in the light.
I do not understand how I could drive
with this stone protruding
from my torso.
Nor do I comprehend
the means to discover
which buses I require in place of my car.
The stone, slick with moisture,
throbs relentlessly in the socket of my belly.
I lower myself in careful stages to sit on the asphalt.
I know I cannot walk
as far as I need to go.

ROY ROBERTS

Fathoms

He works in the engine room of a trawler
maintaining the diesel and shaft,
learning the code of sounds and silences
that gets them out and back.

He's learned to care for himself aboard
but the other guys disappoint him,
drinking and smoking dope too much
and not being enchanted by the splendour
the sea, the mountains, grizzly bears fishing!

(Among them) he misses his girlfriend
"Just sitting, feeling her femininity beside me" he said
looking in my eyes, smiling with his mouth
wondering what I thought of tenderness
unannounced and disheveled,
his eyes and mouth suddenly opened blooms
surprised by light and unable to close.

LUANNE ARMSTRONG

Diving

That bright time
when everyone is there and you
are younger than the day
it's all go go, and bodies pressed against
bodies, toes stuck to
warm granite
gripping air, sun,
shoved
and then
no more
holding, no more

not a decision;
floating in space,
floating
before anything can catch you,
not gravity or desire or the will to
complete
some arching towards that
seductive jade

then the impact
the sliding down
the long cool
silk along your skin

entering
down, the pleasure of
down,
green, infinite, whispering
down,
more down than you can imagine

but already you are choosing
twisting in a gasp of need
an arrow carrying with you
bone and flesh,
whispering, need, need,
until
there is flailing and a stroke, kick

and back into air, dizzy,
from a voyage across so much, so fast,
so unreckoned

a memory you capture
again and again
a frenzy of climbing, falling, climbing
to exhaustion
like an angel child
bright cousin to the sky
there's no stopping you now.

BERYL YOUNG

The Old Print

In the small black and white photograph
my father and mother sit on a tapestry patterned sofa
They do not touch   they are not smiling
My mother has put her arm over the cushion beside her
My Dad's hand rests on the bulldog at his feet
My mother looks young   her mouth turns down
her lean legs are crossed   her hair
is tightly marcelled to her head
My father is handsome   his dark eyes burn
there is a five-o'clock shadow on his cheeks
It doesn't show but my mother is pregnant
Two months later the dog will die when he
jumps out the car window after a rabbit

Why doesn't my father reach to touch his new wife?
Why doesn't she turn and smile at him?
Click   their unhappiness is exposed for all time
My life has begun

JOANNA STREETLY

Nameless

She looks at his hands because they are so beautiful. Too large, but well proportioned. The curve of his fingers against the baby's head. His hands. Her baby.

"She's going to be fine, Louise. Don't worry."

She stares at this nurse, this improbable angel. Except for the hands he should be playing rugby. His shoulders are as wide as the bed her daughter is lying on—and she, so small, like a seed. The nurse has said that his name is Scott, but Louise cannot think of names. In her head he is the nurse; the nurse in charge of her baby's life.

Outside in the hallway there is noise: clattering trolleys, snapping heels, the heaving of double doors, and in the distance, the circling whine of a floor polisher. In her head there is a pool of silence. Louise cannot allow disturbance—stones, ripples, waves. Even the nurse's words float lightly, not penetrating.

She returns her gaze to the tiny mouth, the four pearly new teeth barely visible. Lips slack. Chest moving up, moving down. A mantra. She imagines a seabird, a storm petrel, dipping and flowing over steady grey swells, wings hanging lightly from air.

Louise is willing her child away from death. She has lost to death before. This time she wants a fight. But for now, there is stability. When she first scrabbled through the door, sobbing and incoherent, a thumbtack was blocking the trachea. A silent, rock-eyed baby, mouth like an o, paralysed with confusion.

The nurse was fast. He slapped her tiny back to no avail. Then, grey and quiet, she was on a stretcher, wheeling towards oxygen and other unknowns. They went too fast. The stretcher careened around a corner and slammed hard into the doorway—Bam!—and then the screaming, the baby crying, amazingly breathing. No more silence. Object dislodged, partially.

The baby is wheezing quietly now, not much needed to sedate her. "Doctor's orders," the nurse said as he slid the needle in. "If she moves around too much, it might happen again. We have to find out where it's gone; what we can do." The look of sedation is ghostly; like a premonition.

Another nurse arrives, grey-haired and skirted. White stockings, comfortable shoes. They move the stretcher slowly now, out into the hallway, toward the X-ray department. Louise hovers like a horsefly, ready to bite. She walks distractedly, trying to keep her eyes on the baby's breathing. She remembers the seabird and wills herself back out to the ocean. The lilt of grey water carries her along.

"Louise!" calls a voice. The cavalcade slows as the admitting clerk, Margaret, hurries towards them, clipboard in hand.

"We need your baby's name for the computer. We still

have her down as 'baby girl.' I should have asked you last time, when you came in to have her weighed."

Louise flushes cold and starts to shake. She loses sight of the seabird. Margaret waits, pen poised, head tilted in sympathy. The pause lengthens. No words emerge. The nurses look at her as they slide away—alert, curious, like deer. Louise looks away from Margaret.

"No name," she croaks, then stumbles after the stretcher.

Margaret stands, staring, alone between walls, her reflection glowing dimly in the waxed, green floor.

·↵

The X-ray theatre whirrs and hums with latent danger. Louise thinks of it as a chamber, as if that name could better convey the sense of malice. She has always refused X-rays, preferred not to know. "Well," she thinks to herself, "no moral superiority today." Today is obviously a day for fear and humility. Today she has had to announce, in public, that her nine-month-old baby is nameless. She's not quite sure why there should be shame attached to this, but there is. As if *Sweetie*, *Missy*, *Love* are not enough. She relives the moment. She should have invented a name and made it easier for everyone. They think differently of her now. Even Scott, with his hands so full of love. It's bad enough that her baby has swallowed a tack. The lack of a name pushes Louise over an invisible line: normal mother; bad mother.

Louise imagines the tiny bones of her baby's neck and the angular point of metal. Will the tack be a blur on the X-ray? she wonders. Does it move every time air goes in?

She resumes her watch of the breathing. Steady. She thinks of her other babies, the ones she jinxed by naming them. They never breathed this way. They took air from her body—well, Nina never took very much of anything. She was the first of the never-born babies, and the most short-lived. She passed through Louise's legs at seven weeks, when Louise was just twenty. Hardly time to get to know her. And then she was blood. And pain. And Louise on her own, in the bathroom at the college library, hoping no one would notice. Hoping that the worst would pass before the library closed and the doors were locked.

January 20, 1989.

In a way it was a relief. She wanted to get her degree and she hadn't told Stephen yet. He'd always been good to her, but she knew he'd freak at the idea of a baby. He was in the chemistry lab when it happened, one building away, doing an experiment.

She did well in her exams that year, as if the miscarriage showed her what she should want in life: a career, not a family—well, not yet, anyway. She could never explain why she had welcomed that baby so much. It didn't fit any of her goals. It wasn't as if she went to university to get pregnant. But from the start she had thrilled with the knowledge of her pregnancy, reached orgasm to the vision of an open cervix, warm womb, sperm meeting egg. Her hands obsessed about the baby they could not feel, sliding over her abdomen, in a constant figure of eight. She never considered an abortion. She never told Stephen. Not even afterwards. "Period pains," she shrugged. "This month's a brute."

Mary-Anne was Jeff's kid. Or would have been. She was stronger, clung on for three months. Louise and Jeff were engaged at the time. Babies weren't on the agenda, but it was okay. Jeff had a good job, could support a family. He didn't mind about the baby. But he didn't mind about the miscarriage, either. Not the way Louise did. He didn't feel the pain or the hot clumpy blood.

"Are there any products of conception?" the ambulance man had asked her. As if she could respond to words like that.

March 17, 1993.

.ے

The nurse, Scott, chats with the X-ray technician, keeping an eye on the little girl. He keeps an eye on the mother, too. She's standing by the stretcher with shoelace strands of hair and zombie eyes. Shock. She hasn't spoken much. It's normal, but you have to keep an eye out. She could keel over any minute.

Earlier, while he was rushing around, Scott ordered up the baby's chart. On impulse, he ordered the mother's, too. The birth chart showed that this was her fourth pregnancy. She'd miscarried all the rest. This baby's life was a long time coming. He thinks of his own boys, aged two and five, woven into his body fibres. Possessive love flows out of him. It's easy to love this little girl, too.

Nursing has taught Scott to avoid emotional attachments to his patients, but from time to time the shield slips and he finds himself enmeshed. This is one of those occasions. He feels as if he has slipped into a multi-dimensional world, like a dream, where he cannot separate himself from the players. He is them and they are him. A voice instructs him, tells him how to act. He trusts the voice; recognizes his professional persona.

"You won't lose her," he tells Louise. "She's an old soul. Strong. She wants this world."

Louise stares at him, pupils slightly uneven.

"I should have told her father."

"Do you want to use the phone?"

"I don't know where he is." Her voice has slowed. She speaks in a questioning tone. Scott wonders what kind of a relationship Louise has with the baby's father. Love goes wrong so easily.

"You'll be able to find him," Scott reassures her. "This will be over soon. It'll be fine, I know."

"You don't understand."

⸰⸱

In a city, worlds away, Jeff escapes from his office. He breathes in the sharp spring air and the sudden exhaust of a passing car. At the coffee shop, Hilda asks him if he wants the usual. He smiles, puts the coins on the counter. It's good to be a regular.

He takes the cappuccino over to the window seat, a plush chair that is seldom vacant. He's lucky today. His body sags into the chair. Life has changed so much: new town, new job, new girlfriend, new image. He's a corporate cowboy now, not a frantic, sweaty small businessman. Gone are the baggy sweaters, piles of bills, tiptoed steps around his home office. Living with Louise was like living in a morgue. After the miscarriages, she had never been the same. He couldn't understand it, really. He wanted kids, too, but a couple of miscarriages weren't the end of the world. They could have adopted.

Well, kids aren't really in the cards for him, now. Jessica's only twenty-four, with a busy life of her own. They meet in the evenings for drinks, movies, the occasional night club.

Jeff breathes in the thick scent of espresso, almost better than the coffee itself. He slurps a mouthful of foam, but a hot splash of liquid hits the back of his throat and sets him coughing. Tears squeeze out of his eyes. He puts the cup down and dabs at his tie, hoping to escape a stain. The coughing fit raises looks of alarm from the other patrons.

"It's okay!" he manages, between ragged breaths, to the woman next to him. She leans back and continues searching her briefcase, eventually pulling out a sheaf of papers. Something about her reminds him of Louise. Perhaps it is the reading glasses.

He's breathing normally again now. Not quite ready for another stab at the coffee, but he will be soon. He looks at the woman again. She is radiating some kind of happiness, sureness, calm. He tries to pin it down, but he can't. It's how Louise seemed just before he left. As if she had been set to rights. The cloud of depression had lifted, revealing the sweet soul he first fell in love with. He knew it wouldn't last.

The woman next to him snaps her briefcase shut. Jeff realizes that it's time for him to go, too. He'll fit a lid onto his coffee and take it back to the office with him. He smiles at the woman as he rises and she smiles back, before bending to pick up her briefcase. As she stands, he notices the swell of her breasts and the curve of her belly. He's amazed he didn't see it before. She is pregnant, probably about halfway through. He tries not to stare, but his mouth drops open.

He sits back down and shifts his eyes to the window. He'll be late back to work, but, suddenly, he's got a lot on his mind.

SHANNON COWAN

The Woman in This Story

The woman in this story is lying in bed, awake, under a single white sheet stiff with sizing. Her mouth is dry and her hands smell of barley cereal, the last meal she attempted to feed her child who is now sleeping fitfully in the next room. Every five minutes her child murmurs in the darkness, rolls her soft, hot body from the middle of her mattress—where the woman positioned her the last time she coaxed her to sleep—to the grill of the safety bar where she bangs her head, then lets out a sleep-starved, angry cry. If the cry persists, turns into a shout—the sound of her child rising, pulling herself up onto the bars of the crib—the woman rushes to the nursery and places her hand on the child's forehead, checks the burn of fever, the slick of sweat, sings the refrain from Simon and Garfunkel's "For Emily, Wherever I May Find Her," and then eases her child back into the newly flattened bedding where—in her tossing—she had built a knot of blankets. After she is sure her child has passed, for the moment, into the shallow surfaces of sleep, the woman walks the narrow apartment hallway to the living room to see if her husband has come home and crawled onto the couch, to check the red indicator light on the telephone answering machine that flashes on and off if a call has been missed. When she confirms there is neither a husband nor a message, she parts the louvred blinds across the living-room window, parts them with a shake of dust onto the clipped acrylic rug to see if he is asleep in the driveway inside their sapphire Plymouth Sundance—his size 14 feet curled into the armrests in a squeeze of exhaustion— or to see if an ambulance or police cruiser is there instead. After this round of surveillance from bed to baby to couch to window, the woman returns to her room and listens on the edge of her mattress, on the edge of sleep, watching the numbers of her digital clock flipping swiftly towards morning.

·~

Most people—when they find themselves in a situation of not knowing—try not to expect the worst. The woman in this story cannot, for any reason, conjure up an excuse for her husband that does not involve broken bones, spontaneous combustion, jagged cliffs, the Jaws of Life, transport trucks careening into oncoming lanes. She can't imagine him safe, so refuses to call the hospital, the local detachment of police, as a way of preserving—at least for now, at least in her own mind—her husband's life. It is in this not knowing that he still has a chance, that his death remains an overreaction, a drastic, overwrought conclusion arrived at by someone who has not considered all the possibilities. She tries instead to focus on her baby—a child she loves with ferocity and tenderness, a child who has changed her life, her body, irreversibly, by christening her in motherhood—but she can't stop thinking about her husband, who complicated things in the first place; her doctor, who told her she was as sterile as a dust bowl; and herself for listening and losing track of ovulation, disposing of dial-packs, diaphragms, flushing condoms down the toilet. And despite the love she feels for her child, her husband, her aging parents, she wants for one minute to be free of other people's pain, their potential deaths and abandonments, their surgeries, their cancers, their slow lapses into dementia, so she can care about herself and remember why she is here. And while she wishes this she simultaneously knows she is not serious, feels guilt, retracts those thoughts in favour of what she really wants which is her husband, her baby, both of them sleeping soundly beside her, long into the morning.

·ك

The man in this story is driving home in a sapphire Plymouth Sundance purchased with a borrowed down payment and no interest for five years. His eyes droop in their sockets, threatening to shut out the instrument panel, the ruins of the Britannia mine, an adjacent tourist teahouse, the narrow winding highway and its hundred-foot drop to Howe Sound below; threatening to close him instead into the dark confusion of his dreams, where children stray onto busy streets and the man himself is forced back into elementary school, into his grade six classroom desk, despite his present age of twenty-nine. To keep himself awake, he thinks about his baby who has not slept for three nights because of the first pain of teeth; about his wife, a woman he has loved since graduating from university, but whom—he has determined—he cannot deserve or ever understand; about how he wants to do better, get home earlier, but was kept back by the man in charge of his raise and his promotion who informed him—as they walked from an out-of-town meeting to the parking lot—that he was considering suicide. Viewing everything in a blur of sleep deprivation, the man in this story turned to his colleague, saw his tight, starched face bent on deadlines slacken for the first time. He heard his own voice, strangely melodious, saying into the chill of deep night, "Do you want to talk about it?"

Once you have offered yourself up—even to a man who is unlikeable, crass, rough; even to a man that you have avoided since your first year of university because, in the darkness of the university pub, he tried to kiss your girlfriend—you are obligated to listen. The man in this story knew of this obligation and sat down with his colleague on the edge of the sea to listen to a lifetime of mistakes: of exam cheating and divorce proceedings, of drug experimentation and custody battles, of harassment and medication, of rejection, compulsion, addiction and loss. He was losing, this other man; he was at the end of his rope. The man in our story, although half-awake, although red-eyed and distracted by the drip of a runny nose, leaned forward when the other man finished and gave him some advice. He spoke aloud, his voice crackling with the fissures of another day, words of sage advice he had not used in his own life, words that came from who knows where. He heard these words and realized his position of relative light and strength, his life of small successes equalling one big success. He heard his confident, measured voice opening up a cask of ancient secrets, truths to live by, and decided, from that moment forward, to live by them too. He brought the man back to his car and then slid into his own. He turned onto the highway at the confluence of the Squamish and Cheakamus Rivers where spawning salmon fought their way upstream. He headed for home.

The last time the woman in this story spoke to her husband, she reminded him of his mother's birthday. She reminded him with a pinch in her voice, with patience distended from so many years of remembering for him. She reminded him by placing a calendar on the table, by pointing to the date—circled in lurid green—and then recalling aloud his past five years of forgetting when she, his wife and not even really related to the mother, rushed to the stationer's at the last possible moment and attempted to select, from the racks marked *Parental Birthday*, the kind of card a mother would expect from her son.

The last time the man in this story spoke to his wife, he sat at the kitchen table, a melamine-oak combination with a scratched, bleached surface, and stared at his hands. He fought a rise of defeat and unworthiness rolling out from his eyes and cheeks, from his chest and forehead, spreading across his face and into the kitchen in a slow and angry silence. He followed this with the statement, "I'll remember this year. I'll do it today," then picked up his lunch and headed out the door.

A lie, the woman thought this morning when her husband spoke about remembering his mother's birthday. A lie, she thinks now, as she stalks into the nursery trying to recall his eyes, the way they moved away from her own and searched instead for the fridge, the window, for someone who would understand that even though he may have been lying, he did it for everyone's benefit; that even though he may have been lying, it was all that he could do. He was acting out a pattern, her husband, rising late every morning of the year, coming to breakfast with shaving cream still on his chin, mumbling through a meal of toast and jam and only enough time for one cup of coffee, then fleeing into the early dawn, his shirt untucked, his leather oxfords stained with dew, chasing the bus down to Phibbs Exchange and across the bridge to his office where he would sit quietly behind an office divider and forget all about his mother's birthday. She was acting out a pattern too, the woman in this story. Everything she knows and despises about patterns tells her that her ill-timed responses, her own weary role as the let-down upset wife is part of the problem. She thinks about this as she forces the tip of a plastic dropper between the lips of her crying baby, her hands sticky with banana-flavoured syrup, her eyes swollen and red-rimmed in the glow of the nursery nightlight.

.⸗

Most people, when they are unexpectedly late, call whomever may be waiting for them and tell them not to worry. Most people, when they are unexpectedly late, imagine themselves in the waiter's shoes, anxious, alone, pacing in front of the clock. By the time the man in this story returns to the road, he can think only of his wife still in her housecoat, finally asleep in the warm envelope of their bed, grabbing a few hours before the baby wakes and demands mashed cherries and seven ounces of formula cooled to room temperature. He can think only of his parents, their anger descending on him like an anvil, when he brought home the wrong grades, the wrong woman, when he forgot them at birthdays and Christmas and sent instead a box of chocolates, poorly wrapped in recycled tissue paper, two weeks late. He can think only of a series of nights, days, mornings and afternoons, when he decided to call or not to call, when he decided to make a decision. For it is not simply three nights without sleep that persuade him to do nothing, but the idea that no matter what he does, he will be wrong, he will be making the wrong decision, and therefore doing nothing is just as well.

Instead of sleeping as her husband imagines, the woman in this story sits on top of a thinning coverlet and looks at the pictures in their wedding album, pictures she mounted with vinyl adhesive triangles onto acid-free paper and then divided using layers of vellum: the woman, open and smiling, teeth just visible between parted lips, standing three inches taller than her husband because of borrowed heels and an arrangement of plaits on top of her head garnished with yellow roses; the woman and her bridesmaids, two close friends and a scarcely known paternal cousin, squinting into the afternoon sun, the ocean behind them blue as flax and dotted with sailboats; her mother- and father-in-law, lounging on church pews complaining of heat, overspiced chicken, the lack of after-dinner sherry or vodka or anything hard to chase the fruitcake; the rushed afternoon ceremony quickened to eliminate the embarrassment of new, drunk relatives. "I don't care what they're like," the woman had said to her husband. "They're your parents. Invite them." She smoothes her fingers over the edges of the photos, marvelling at what she knows now that she did not know on her wedding day: that the man in the photo, after he became her husband, would still leave rings in the bathtub; that she would still lose her temper, sometimes crying over stains in the laundry; that they would still argue over money, dirty frying pans, unmade beds, missed anniversaries now rendered official by the rings on their fingers; that she and her husband, that both of them, would still be the same people as the ones in the photographs, despite a lack of satin, of tuxedo, of pearls and wine and boutonnieres; and that although they still loved each other, maybe now more than ever, maybe even more than that, they would still not be able to get along. And instead of sleeping, the woman flips through her wedding album, imagining what life would be like if they could.

·ے

Somewhere between five and six in the morning the woman in this story falls asleep on top of the covers, her legs crossed at the ankles, her head falling into the cloud of the feather pillows propped behind her shoulders. In her brief slumber she misses the click of the exterior door, the quiet removal of size fourteen oxfords and their brief scattering on the door-mat, the sigh of second-hand couch cushions as they bend under the weight of a body relaxing into the upholstery. She misses all this and wakes with a start, reading the morning light as it seeps between the divide in her bedroom curtains, the red numbers on her digital clock displaying 6:15, and sprints to the front hall to see the mound of her husband turned to the wall. "What happened?" she says in a low voice, tugging at her robe. "Where have you been?" Her husband rolls over and blinks at the ceiling. "What?" he says, not yet awake. Then, "Nothing, I was talking to some-one from work." "I thought you were dead," says the woman, her voice rising. "Anything could have happened." She stops talking when she hears the baby cry, her face tight on the edge of tears. "You are so selfish," she says, and then stalks back down the hallway, wondering why she is back where she started, how she got there in the first place.

The man looks at the ceiling, wondering half in sleep, half in reality, about the conversation from the night before, unable to recall his words of sage advice, unable to remember anything but his own tired voice, the sound of his throat closing.

ALEXANDER FORBES

Baltasar Carlos

what it must be like to be
a child and know yourself

heir apparent to the King of Spain—
then be summoned by the nursemaid who
will lead you for a time, until the day
she will be forbidden to know you any
longer: the girl who now shuffles you
past the dwarf who had once been your
companion, until you reach the studio of

Velázquez—
where you will sit impatiently for
another portrait to carry your likeness
into the future, until you are returned
to the nursery where you will stare from
your window upon Madrid and its plain
only to fear the day when you too will be

a heavy King of Spain like your father—
if you do not die before him, as you will

KATE BRAID

Lullaby for a Sick Father

Papa, as I stand over your bed I close my eyes
and dream back to construction days, feel
the grain of my fingers, their memory
of pitch and sawdust, and wish
that trees could move for you

and it is so.

In darkest night, a British oak, sweet cedar,
a powerful Douglas fir and the graceful arbutus
shift, stand quietly now
at the four corners of your hospital bed.

You are already small
as they extend their roots
gently, meet and form a net
beneath you. No one notices
as your hospital bed lifts
one leg then another until
as though in a hammock
you sway, a child again, rocking.
You are not alone.
Four guardians, posted at the corners
of your heart-heightened world
lift, their humming lives transferred
like a current, their pulse now pounding for yours.

Do you feel it, a transfusion of nectar and green?
You settle and sigh into a swaying peace,
given breath drawn deep from earth, from sky.
Birds come.
There is a small cutting and travelling of beetles,
the whisper of bud, flower, leaf,
a breeze of fervent green.

You dream
deep handholds of bark, your strength
the smooth arms of arbutus and you rest,
in greatness. No matter what happens now
you are safe.

DAVID WATMOUGH

The Naturalist

He sat in the skimpy shade of the arbutus on the headland, watching two sea otters play one hundred feet beneath him. He'd been there since sun-up—his favourite time—and by now, three hours later, his bum was beginning to throb. Last week, at the same hour, he had been deep in the woods behind him, watching a black bear and her two cubs from his Douglas fir perch, and long before the cubs had tired of their play and followed her into the brush, he knew the mosquitoes had drunk a bloody banquet off him. Then, as he told himself proudly, he was a naturalist and such were the prices one paid. There was a scar on his right index finger, born many springs back, when he was attempting to liberate a young long-tailed weasel that was entrapped by a log along the beach.

He was also only three-foot-eleven and that fact was more than he could sometimes endure. It was certainly more persistent than insect bites and an aching posterior.

As usual, when straying towards that particular mental territory, he grew restless. Stared for relief once more down the cliff face at the roiling surf below. Or rather, at the sand which prefaced it and which—freshly gleaming narrow strand though it was—had suddenly become the home to a variety of seabirds: primarily mergansers and flocks of turnstones.

So keen was he to concentrate on this teeming life of the coast, he was almost tempted to start counting the birds as they alighted in piping agitation and then darted hither and thither along the seaweed-strewn sand. He knew, though, from experience, that this was a useless quest. The turnstones particularly, were so manic in their maneuvers that their sudden return to flight or abrupt dive back to earth made numerical estimation impossible. They were as mysterious, unfathomable, in their avian way over their abrupt change of purpose as those thundering herds of African wildebeest pursued by predators—much like he'd often seen on his TV screen before switching off such animal programs, suspecting their motives pandered primarily to appetites for the subsequent kill and resultant gore.

Then he was back to the domestic world of his TV viewing and the antics of turnstones failed to protect him. What was it that Leonard, his next-door neighbour, had said when he was hanging his hummingbird feeder in the apple tree? "Danny, if you hang it *that* low all you'll be doing is feeding the local cats!"

As if Leonard and his partner, Richard, knew a fuck about hummingbirds! *Any* kind of birds for that matter. They were gays and probably knew a lot about interior decorating and that was that. Not that Danny thought for one moment that his nosy neighbour was really alluding to the

April return of the rufous hummingbird. Oh no, that reference was to the fact that without getting a ladder or resorting to the help of the likes of him, that young Leonard was speaking only of his neighbour's own height, or lack of it, and thus being as bitchy as the rest of 'em—in spite of the fact that queers lived in equally fragile glass houses and should act accordingly.

He had told his wife, Edna, about the incident as soon as he'd gone back inside and asked her to hold the stepladder as he reluctantly climbed it to tie the feeder in a safer place. But she—she of the same height as he—was no comfort. Forty years earlier, when they'd met in California, they had been total in their solidarity as "Little People"—a term they had both helped to popularize as an advocacy group for their kind. But since their sixties things had changed. She no longer was all support. Why should she be? he sometimes asked himself. He had given her the distinguished reputation of being married to a published naturalist to lean on and—he less often conceded—she had built up a substantial reputation as a potter whose ceramics had grown progressively in demand, not only there in Vancouver but in cities to the south such as Seattle, Portland, and even San Francisco.

Of course, those remote buyers had no idea of the diminutive hands that had created the ceramics they'd purchased—any more than his readers would have known of his own physical stature. Then as a woman, living now in their comparative isolation, with her kiln downstairs and the people along the Sunshine Coast knowing and admiring her skill for a number of years, life had become considerably smoother, more palatable for her.

Why not then for him? Danny asked. Asked more now at sixty-five than he had as a young man when he was persistently mistaken for a child or—worse—as some kind of malevolent freak from whom real children ran with their fear permeating their shrill voices. That was when he wasn't being consigned exclusively to the employment of circuses and sideshows.

"Half the time, you imagine these things, Danny. You know very well that neither Leonard nor Richard would ever say anything malicious. Leonard was just thinking of the hummingbirds while you, dear, were thinking of your own comfort.

"You forget things so quickly, Danny. Like the first time we had dinner over there and Leonard told us that when they'd moved up here people first thought they must be waiters or actors or something. And you told them about my pottery and your own books and that."

Danny wasn't disposed to argue with her. Why get her curly white head all fussed up with the kind of thing he damn well knew happened to him, and which she'd only do her best to deny, even if she saw it happen.

Then of course she never did. We see only what we want, he reflected. And Mrs. Edna Bernardi nowadays only saw a rather diminutive but distinguished couple who had come to live in late middle-age, here on the outskirts of Sechelt, where both could pursue their professional activities without the distractions of a big city like Vancouver.

Well, at least they were free of all that, he told himself for the umpteenth time, as he prepared to vacate his improvised "blind" up there on the clifftop now that all the thoughts,

regrets, and frustrations connected to his physical self, and
to a progressively uncomprehending wife, had started to get
to him.

He made his way down past the clumps of alder and red
elderberry that succeeded the stands of pine and arbutus,
through the—for him—tall clumps of skunk cabbage (he
preferred the name of "swamp lantern")—a secret route
that taller people would never have discovered and of which
even Edna knew nothing—to that flat immensity of sea and
land that dwarfed all mankind and of which he knew so
much more than most.

Where he emerged—out of a sea of bramble and gorse
where he often encountered browsing blacktail deer and
marauding raccoons—he breathed in deeply. Partly because
the steep descent had made his little body breathless, but
partly out of appreciation of the scene confronting him.
Looking down from above had a pleasing, panoramic effect
for him but it lacked the dimensions of smell and sound that
he now obtained in full measure. Long gone was any sense
of the actual number of times he had stood there, taking in
the briny pungency of the Pacific, the nervous fingers of
breeze that pushed insistently from the southwest, and, of
course, the constant sibilance of the undulating tide.

Today there was a bonus: a visual one. Ambling towards
him, probably headed for the neighbouring creek and its
entering salmon, was a mother black bear and her two cubs.
He stood perfectly motionless, glad that he was downwind
of them. None knew better than Danny from years of pro-
tracted observation, of the poor sight but keen scent and
hearing of *Euarctos americanus*. He was convinced that it

was the same family he'd watched on the earlier occasion. There was a nick in the sow's ear and her colouration was surely identical—noteworthy in a species where there was considerable variation.

It was the cubs that captivated his attention. He considered himself a scientist and impervious to the nudges of anthropomorphism when confronting the playful charm of young wild animals such as that of these bears, or scampering raccoon kits. Even so he felt his heart give an uncontrolled thump. The gamboling about their mother as she plodded steadfastly towards her unknown destination of the two animated balls of dark brown fur was, he knew, part of their intricate preparation for maturity and survival. But there was surely a pleasure in their play as well as an innocence that brought them forcibly into the human orbit of identifying affection.

With Danny it went further—and he knew it. As he warmed to their grunting, squealing presence he correspondingly felt a personal lacuna. Edna and he had no children. They had tried. They had seen gynecologists, obstetricians, sex counsellors, and attended several fertility clinics. He had even done personal research into the sexual potential of those having mutual hypoplasia. But the end result was the commonplace situation wherein he was sexually fertile but Edna incapable of childbirth. They had grieved over that for many months, perhaps a year, before contemplating adoption. But there it was she who was willing to explore the matter and he who grew progressively opposed. He was ashamed to tell her, but he found himself emotionally incapable of facing the possibility of rejection. A rejection, maybe, by some stupid, ill-educated young woman who had conceived a baby and now wanted rid of it—but balked at the idea of it going to dwarves. That he would not, could not contemplate. He had learned to tolerate so much by the time he was in his thirties and had met and married Edna.

So they moved on in life without the presence of babies; no smell of talcum, let alone of diapers, no infant gurgles, wails or screams. No later problems of education or watching one's children turn into adolescents and then into adults. Only the trouble was that while Danny had been able to firmly put the ideas of adoption behind him, just as he'd resolved the immediate disappointment of them being unable to have their own offspring—the hunger for the impedimenta of parenthood never left him for a moment. Never let up. Indeed when he saw others with their children or—yes, even a humble bear with her cubs—the slumbering ache in his side was wide awake again. He wasn't only a pathetic diminutive of his species but was unable to contribute to the human future by the transference of love, guidance, and the richness of vision he had harvested as a naturalist. He had held orphaned bear cubs, knew the sharp needles of their claws as he allowed them to climb all over him as they would shin up the bark of a tree. As the family now passed him, unaware or oblivious of his presence (he wasn't sure which) he could also imagine the hot, fruity smell of their breath.

When they were gone he found his eyes blurred. He wiped them and looked with fresh determination at the seabirds feeding at the edge of the tide. He drew in breath with such force—longing as he did to draw olfactory sustenance for his questing nostrils—that he was tempted to sneeze. Instead he left his cover and carefully maneuvered his small body between the piled logs at the top of the beach and made his way towards the further headland where he knew he could listen to the staccato calls of his beloved belted kingfishers (on whom he'd written his first published treatise) and perhaps a glimpse of those giant Steller's sea lions which he believed were becoming more and more common along that stretch of coast. This was not the time of year their pups would be in evidence.

He'd reached halfway down the beach between the cliffs he'd left and the dribbling surf when he thought he heard a shout and turned his head towards the sky-line of untidy arbutus. He could see no one. There was one uneasy moment when, remembering he was wearing his khaki shorts below his bright check shirt, he recalled being mistaken for an unattended boy, about to wander too close to a perilous ocean.

He threw the notion off, laughed into the breeze. Now he could see fragments of dead crab and other tidal flotsam that shared the attention of the glaucous-winged gulls that wheeled and screamed their hungry presence.

Now he was at home, *truly* at home, and a welcome warmth came back into him in spite of the stiffening wind, in spite of the fact that his climbing boots eventually reached the water, became covered by the tide that was very soon mounting and lapping between his thighs . . .

W.H. NEW

Walkmen

The others—a dozen 17-year-olds
on a trip to the crater, all wired in
headphones—smile on the way past,
how ya doin, hi, scrambling
down from the summit, muster the
static manners they mostly
keep for strangers, *good morning sir, hello—*
it means they're unafraid, chattering
games, groups, cameras—

does it, like, focus by itself?—

the boy with jug ears, though,
feet flapping on the pumice,
doesn't even see you hiking by: *he's*
too busy following the kids in *front*,
trying to keep *up*, his mind
fastened on what they're *saying*,
what he *thinks* they're saying,
being one of *them*, & not
the boy with jug ears—

JUDY MCFARLANE

Signs of the Mind

At first, she doesn't mind. After all, it keeps him busy. He walks through the kitchen, past the small entry hall, into the living room, back out, and into the kitchen again. He is wearing his old slippers with the split toes, the ones that make the sound of fine sandpaper as he moves slowly across the linoleum. He must have passed through the kitchen ten, fifteen times now. He hasn't said anything, just looked at her and nodded. She sees that his breathing is slightly ragged. His cheeks puff out in a small, barely noticeable way, as if he is getting ready for something bigger. Next time around, she thinks, she'll ask him to stop, stay with her in the kitchen, have a cup of tea.

The light is always the same, he thinks. A sharp, clean light, hot and searing. Through the window, he sees it glint off the windshields of the parked cars. So hot, he thinks, always so hot. Which way to the river? It's down the hill, but which way? There's a path, Dick somewhere ahead of him, calling back, "Come on Eddie, come on!" Dick's always ahead of him, leading, taking his role as older brother seriously. But where's Dick now? He turns the corner, holding the smooth edge of the wall, and he's in a kitchen now. Keep going, he thinks, keep going. Smile, the woman is baking something.

She lightly lifts the pastry and rotates it on the floured counter. She pushes the rolling pin quickly across it and then lifts the pastry into the glass pie plate. Tenderly, she eases the pastry into the plate, pushing it up and over the edge. With one hand, she balances the plate near eye level. With the other, she deftly cuts the excess dough in one swift motion, sees it drape momentarily over her arm, then fall in creamy folds to the counter. She loves the pastry, its elasticity, its floury richness, the way she can make it stand up in a perfect ruffled edge around the rim of the pie plate. She lets her hands linger on the dough as if she is caressing it. For a moment, she feels as if everything is normal. Ed will stop soon and she will say, "Come on, let's sit down," and they will have a cup of tea together as they always have. She lifts her hands slowly from the pastry and looks around. What has she done with the filling? The apple slices are coated with a film of cinnamon and brown sugar, sitting in her old white bowl. Where is it?

He's in the kitchen again. He feels his breath catching slightly. He stops and puts one hand out against the fridge. Just be a moment, he thinks, I won't be long. Should he call to Dick? He hasn't seen him for a while now. Is he already down at the riverbank? He feels his breath start to even out. His hand can feel the humming vibration of the fridge. He turns to look at it. There's something stuck to the fridge, a paper taped across the front of it. He looks at the words carefully:

WE SOLD OUR HOUSE
WE LIVE HERE NOW
THIS IS OUR HOME

She didn't think of the sign until the day Ed turned on her. She had snapped at him after he had asked her, for the tenth time in as many minutes, what had they done with the house. Where were they now? He had glared at her with an accusing look, as if she had somehow spirited the house away when he wasn't looking.

"Who the hell do you think you are?" he'd snarled. "Who are you to tell me what to think?" His face red and dry-looking, his eyes staring past her to something behind her. He had slammed his hand across the counter, sending the plate flying, in a short heavy curve onto the floor, where it burst into triangular shards. "Leave me alone," he'd muttered, "just leave me alone, goddamn you." And he'd walked heavily out of the kitchen, favouring his knee that bothered him at times.

WE SOLD OUR HOUSE

He stares at the words. He knows what they say. But why? . . . We sold our house? When? A feeling of unease nags at him as he stares at the sign. Maybe if he listens, if he's careful, he'll hear Dick over the sound of the river. Dick will be digging in the gravel at the edge of the river, looking for the perfect rock. Smooth, flat, but heavy enough to throw a long way. Then Dick will lean back, holding the rock in his hand and throw it in a clean line, almost parallel with the water. The rock will arc slightly, then drop in the first of a series of graceful slaps on the surface of the water. Dick will turn and smile at him. "Here," he'll say. "I found one for you," and he'll open his fist to show him another perfect rock.

"Ed," she says, "have you seen my white bowl?" She looks at Ed hopefully. Sometimes he knows who she is and what she's saying. She hangs onto these moments, holding them in her mind long after they are over. "Ed?" she says, more tentatively now. He's staring at her, a look she can't interpret on his face. "Ed?" she says and she hears, to her dismay, a pleading note creep into her voice.

He stops by the counter, takes in the pie plate, the fresh pastry, the flour scattered across the counter, the woman standing in an apron, her floury hands held up to him. There is a feeling he likes here, perhaps he's been here before, in fact, he's sure he has. He nods his head at the woman. Maybe she's seen Dick. Dick looks like him. Some people ask, "Are you twins?" Dick doesn't like that; he wants them to know he's the older brother. He smiles shyly at her. No. She won't know Dick. "Have you seen—?" He stops. Who is he looking for? Is it Dick or—? This woman. "Are you—have you seen my wife?" He's not sure it's the right question, but maybe she can help him.

Once she would have laughed at what Ed has said. Tossed it off with her own joke: "That wonderful woman?" But she has forgotten how to laugh. Now she stares back at Ed. Look at me, she wants to scream. It's been—what— fifty-three, fifty-four years? Don't you know who I am? But she doesn't say any of this, not this time. She moves around the counter to the stove. The oven is on, rising to the right temperature. She opens the oven door. Her white bowl gleams dimly back at her. She smells the sharp scent of heated cinnamon.

"Damn!" she says and lets the oven door slam shut. When did she put her bowl in the oven? She traces her steps backward, but can't remember when she picked up the bowl. She replays her steps again, faster, then slower, but there's a gap, a blank spot she can't fill. She feels an edge of fear, a slight panic swelling inside her. It's only a bowl she thinks. It's not important.

She puts on her worn oven mitts on and opens the oven door again. She gingerly lifts the bowl out with both gloved hands and sets it on a potholder on the counter. Steam rises in a small cloud from the bowl. Ed leans over the counter, his face in the cloud. He closes his eyes for a moment, and a smile spreads across his face, then he straightens up and looks at her.

"Smells good," he says. "Is it for sale?" She takes off an oven mitt and slaps it against Ed's hand. "Ninny."

WE LIVE HERE NOW

Ed stares at the words. Where is here, he wonders. Just where is here? He turns to the woman. She might know. He opens his mouth, then closes it. Here. He thinks he knows. The woman. She's sweeping the flour now, moving the broom with short, abrupt strokes across the floor. Bits of pastry fly up in front of the broom. Ed watches the woman. He thinks he knows her. The way she moves her arms, the way her hands are gripping the broomstick. Hasn't he always known her? He leans back against the counter. Yes. She's . . .

He thinks hard. She's, she's ... He stops. The thought is right there. He knows it. In a moment he'll have it.

She can hardly remember how it used to be. No. That's not right. She can remember, too well. So much lost, she thinks. And he doesn't know. Her hands are in the warm water in the sink. She feels bits of wet pastry slide past her fingers. She's not sure she can continue. The nights that seem to go on forever. Ed waking, shuffling out to the kitchen, putting the electric kettle on the stove, the acrid smell of burning plastic floating through the dark apartment. And the questions, repeated every few minutes. Where am I? When did we sell the house? What happened to the money? Where do we live now? Who are you?

Where did Dick go? He was here and now he's gone. Must still be down at the river. Dick likes it at the river. The fast-flowing water streams past the sand at the edge of the river. Sometimes Dick steps into the icy water and holds out a hand to Eddie. "Don't worry," he says, "I'll hold you." Ed turns to leave the kitchen and raises his hand, giving the woman a quick wave. He sees a look pass over her face, as if she has lost her last good friend. "Cheer up," he wants to say, "It's not so bad."

THIS IS OUR HOME

She sees the words as she pulls the plug from the sink and the water drains noisily. The optimism of her words dismays her now. What was she thinking? That somehow it was possible to make a home even though Ed didn't know where he was? That Ed could adjust to their apartment after being in their house for over forty years? Home, she thinks, isn't where we live anymore. It's a feeling, of comfort, of being safe. Maybe that's what it is. Ed doesn't feel safe. Not here. Not anywhere. She hears him coming around the corner again.

"Tea?" she says, and smiles at him.

"Tea?" he repeats, his voice uncertain. "Here?" He looks at her with his pale blue eyes.

She walks around the counter towards him. "Here," she says, taking him in her arms. She senses him pull back and then she feels a tiny relaxing, a softening of him against her. She feels his badly shaven chin move slowly against her ear.

"Yes," he whispers to her. She feels his head move closer to hers, as if he has found a place where he might rest for a moment.

TANA RUNYAN

Tall and Green

for Tygh

Tonight you sit at the wheel trembling
after an indifferent wind
slammed your van broadside,
took you like a sail
toward the watery horizon
where your belief in control,
the solid stone of it, dissolved
in terror at the bottom of your gut.
This is the night when you feel
the ground beneath your wheels
soften to flesh
become the drowning-wound.

And from the wound
your young friend's face
floats upon the roadside. You see him
face down on the garage floor,
the garden hose, a clutched stalk
of green, snaking its way
into the tailpipe of an idling car.

You drive north toward home,
navigate the perilous road at night,

whose icy flanks will carry you
into the cedar-dark forest
where your every sorrow stands
tall and green.

I know this highway also
and when you call collect
from a land so vast it swallows echoes,
I let your tears fill my ears to brimming
and tell you what I know:
find a room someplace safe,
eat something warm,
take a hot shower and curl up in bed.
Remember the Christmas when you were three
and still believed. Know there is a porch light
left on for you and it will burn
all through the night.

BETSY WARLAND

the slit

from the suite "Not Winter, Not Spring"

the sorrow of near-spring,
who writes of this?

how with vanishing snow, the litter &
refuse of our negligence lay bare.

how between still-white & song-filled green, so many who
doggedly endured; decline. decline.

how windows & doors remain sealed & shut
though the air moist-cool; the light so tender —

the sorrow of near-spring,
who writes of this?

in a dream
the white whales swim close to me, unafraid

the prehistoric frog
i thought to be a giant rock

shifts, opens the slit of its mouth
sings a delicate, antediluvian tune

GAIL JOHNSTON

Bilingual

for Catriona & Alvaro

They slip in and out
of Spanish

like otters

in and out
of water

swiftly as birds

take to the air
their supple linguistic

transitions spelling privacy

even in public
intimacy

wherever they desire

each murmured word a subtle caress
every utterance a kiss

two tongues in one mouth

turning
language

into love

ANNE MILES

Close Encounter

In the meadowland above the highway
still, silent, almost invisible
in dusk the doe stands wondering
at us. When we see her we stop
we go as still as she.
Slow then, she walks into the open
hesitant, tip-toe, like a woman in high heels.
She wonders at us, as I said
stares, flicks an ear
circles us, with circles that grow smaller
as if she would approach
but no, she circles.
When we move, she backs off
several yards, but does not run away.
We go down a path through the low brush.
Turning, we find she's followed.

Eventually, Janet comes
along the road with great galumphing dogs.
She calls them back, but already
swift as no high-heeled woman could be
the doe has leapt away and lost
herself among the folded hills.

LORNE DUFOUR

High Anne Bye Anne

It was always like that
one moment she is walking bye
the next moment she is gone

The van broke down
within a mile of her place
I rolled it down her lane

Anne was home
she hooked herself
around the door

Just her eyes were visible
she handed me the phone
disappeared into the house

Later after I hitched
twice into town she helped me
jump the van

She kept saying
I must go, I have no time
for you, for helping you

She was wearing a blue skirt
in the middle of summertime
on the Cottonwood road

I have designs to do
I'm awaiting important calls
I really can't help you

The wind kept tugging
at her skirt, she looked
like the wind owned her

A.S. PENNE

The Forest, The Trees

When Ben talks about his dark theory of love, she is not really listening. She's swallowed up by his eyes, as dark brown as a deer's, liquid and deep. She thinks how she could swim in them if he'd let her.

"We fall in love with people who don't love us back," he says. "And *they* usually want someone who doesn't want them either. It's some kind of karmic joke or something."

She smiles, but not at his words. She is studying his eyelashes, the way they curl as thick as the undergrowth in the forest behind her house.

Ben gives her a look full of chagrin. "It's always the dweebs—the ones we could care less about—that fall in love with us." He shakes his head and looks out the window at the ocean.

Ben is one of her new neighbours, living with his widowed mom since his recent divorce. They met on the beach nearby and ever since then he's been visiting her in the evenings, walking down the street to sit and talk for hours about his ex-wife and his kids. She listens and makes appropriately sympathetic noises because she knows that after all the anger has blown over, Ben will need someone to help him heal. What she's thinking is that maybe when that happens, the two of them can get together, go somewhere.

He does things to touch her without even realizing it. One Sunday he shows up with his chainsaw, ready to fall a dead tree in her yard. He arrives dressed in his work clothes: logger's hardhat, eye goggles, those too-short jeans with the lead-lined legs held up by orange Husqvarna suspenders and leather work gloves. And while he operates the saw, she observes the pure maleness of his body: the dark shadow of beard, unshaved because it is the weekend; the strain of muscle on his thighs and buttocks and the hard ridge of abdominal wall beneath his t-shirt. It is all she can do not to go to him, touch his arm so he'll shut down the saw and she can drag him inside.

But her fantasies are interrupted by real life. In the midst of the screaming chainsaw, Ben's mother walks up the road to watch with her. They chat amiably, she and the older woman, each admiring Ben from their own points of view, and the thought enters her head that the scene in her garden is not unlike something from a television sitcom. How else could she be good friends with the mother of a man whose lights she wants to screw out?

·

Today, though, she takes Ben's dark theory and files it away at the back of her mind. She ignores what he says about love and follows his stare out the window, thinks about how harsh the water looks out there. She came to this place from the city, wanting to be near the ocean, but now she sees how the steel blue and dark grey of the water opposes the warm green of forest.

·⤵

A month after felling her tree, Ben's conversations shift focus. He begins to tell stories of women coming on to him or of a physical encounter with someone he doesn't really like. Then he tells her about someone in his boss's office, a woman he thinks is pretty hot, and she wonders why he's telling her about his sex life. She wonders why he doesn't offer to make her come instead of telling her about all the women who've made him come and she hopes it's just his clumsy logger's way of flirting.

Now when he calls to say he's coming over, she slips into the bathroom to get ready, puts on some mascara or perfume. She's still listening to all his complaints and stories, but what she really hopes is that she'll get laid.

It's been a decade since her last relationship, followed by a number of sorry little affairs, and the grind of time is working against her. She's not desperate—yet—and anyway, if it comes to that there are already two of those dweebs hanging around her door. No, not desperate, but when she sees Ben standing in the doorway, her heart rate jumps as though she's just had a line of coke or a blast of life.

In spite of the mush her innards turn to when Ben is around, her brains haven't yet completely deterioriated.

Now, listening to his talk about himself and his job and his women and his life, she begins to yawn openly. But whenever she tries to redirect him, steering the conversation towards subjects with emotional reality, Ben turns pointedly away. She finds herself thinking how remarkably one-sided is this relationship, how completely lacking in two-way communication.

She makes two decisions: (1) It doesn't matter that he can't talk as long as he can make love; (2) If he can't make love, then the issue is dead all round. Literally and emotionally, like their conversations.

And once she makes that decision, what happens next is her own fault.

As soon as Ben starts up again, complaining about how hard it is to find a partner, doesn't he deserve someone nice, at least someone to sleep with, she doesn't miss a beat.

"Why can't two friends have sex together?"

At first Ben just looks at her. Then he relaxes, interested, and she releases a soft breath of air.

But it's probably the word "friends" that cinches the proposition, because Ben doesn't do anything without thinking about it first. He keeps sex in its place, relationships in a completely different place.

⸱◡

After that first physical encounter, Ben doesn't come by for a whole week and she finds out again how much more than sex there is to want from a man. Especially a man like Ben, who knows how to build things and who thinks about the way it should be done and who has a drawing power that he isn't even aware of. It's in the way his chest is covered with a thick curly fur and the way he's so tired after a day of physical labour that he falls asleep with one rough hand on a woman's belly, making her feel marked. Or as though he might love her.

She spends that long week full of seething, but when he shows up again she puts on a smile. This time when he leaves, she is restless and unable to focus. She tries walking the length of the beach to calm herself, but halfway along the ocean feels too open, too wide so she climbs the hill behind and heads into the dense greenery of forest. Above the water, she is cocooned by the waving boughs of firs, cedars, hemlocks. Now the overhead sky is a warm green blanket and the tangled growth beneath her feet are the paws of a kitten batting at her boots. She feels captured, safe.

·⌒

She tells herself that what she's done with Ben isn't such a big problem, not unless the Right One comes along. But the guy on the white horse hasn't been seen in almost twenty years and so she makes a resolution: until Mr. Right shows up, Ben will do nicely for the time being.

She replays bits of monologues from Ben's endlessly self-absorbed conversations about his marriage, and she decides that he is not at all as he likes to present himself: cold, tough, heartless. She knows, because she has been witness, that this man can cry and protect, use his hands to make a home and to take it apart. And if he can do all those things, surely there is something more beneath his distant surface.

Without intent, Ben gives her no-occasion gifts and birthday and Christmas cards signed *Love Ben* at the bottom. And she takes these small offerings as proof that love, or a primitive form of it, lurks somewhere below the uncommitted exterior. By now she has completely forgotten the dweeb-factor; how only the wrong kind of people fall in love with him.

·⤴

Now she daydreams about spending her life with Ben. This in spite of the fact that he's made things abundantly clear: he's a logger and all he wants is a good meal on the table at night and a good lay in the bedroom and no hassles from Anywoman about anything. And as if to further undermine her dreams, he phones within a week of starting on a new clearcut and tells her that he's found the local meat market.

·⤴

She tries to ignore how remarkably quiet her friends become when she mentions Ben's name.

"What's in this for you?" they want to know.

It is not a question she wants to ask herself and so she looks away, insinuating that the answer should be obvious. "If you want something enough," she says, "you have to be willing to walk through a minefield for it."

⤳

After a year has passed, it makes no difference whether she turns back or continues to cross the minefield. Either way is just as lethal.

She begins to feel the tight walls of her prison: there is no one to whom she can admit how long it's been since she and Ben have been together, or to share something said in the bedroom the last time he was home, something from which she's constructed a much deeper meaning than intended. This is what it's like to live in a small community, she thinks: sleeping with your neighbour on Friday night then taking his mother to the farmer's market Saturday morning. Doing both without being able to discuss the existence of love.

⤳

The next time Ben comes home, she pushes him. After sex one night, she tells him she loves him.

"Aw, don't," he says, pulling away.

But she holds on to his hand.

"I don't mean I love you and I want to get married, Ben. I just mean you're important to me."

And it's as though the forest has cast a spell on her, the way she still doesn't know how to talk to this man. This time it takes several weeks to persuade Ben that it is safe to come back; it was just her hormones acting up.

⤳

One night she lies in the dark listening to the slowing of their two breaths, the way they change from heavy gasps to steady pants and then a regular in and out of air. She is enjoying just being there with him, feeling the rise and fall of his chest under her ear and the warmth of his bigger, rougher palm against hers and out of nowhere he says:

"Are you happy?"

And because she is afraid that he will change his mind about wanting to know something about her, that then she will have lost an opportunity to connect with him, she rushes to answer.

"Really happy," she nods. Without stopping to wonder; without even checking: *Am I happy?*

She waits for another minute, making her breath more and more shallow, listening to see if his burst of conversation—if that's what it is—will continue, but nothing more comes. Finally, realizing she is holding her breath, she takes a large gulp of air and lifts her head, peering for his face in the dark.

"Why?" she asks.

But the moment is gone. He's already sitting up and reaching for his socks.

⁙

In the cold of the open doorway she stands to receive his goodnight hug and then he walks away. She stares up at the black sky pricked with stars, listening for the slam of the gate that says he is gone.

Then she burrows into the tangle of sheets on her empty

bed and in the dark of her room she replays that fleeting moment.

Are you happy?

And with those words, an unbidden image comes to mind: a drive in her father's car when she was very small, a stop at the candy store, and that same question afterwards, *Are you happy now?* Asked in a peeved tone.

She closes her eyes, shakes her head. Surely Ben's question meant, "Do I make you happy?"

And from a tangle of memories comes his earlier prediction: *The people we love never love us back.*

URSULA VAIRA

Love Spell: How to attract a man

For the three days
before full moon
allow only water
to pass your lips
Imagine a stream
trickling over pebbles
the clean scent of moss

On the third night
cleanse your body
in a steaming bath
Imagine the pores
of your skin
opening like stars
in a blue sky

Do not get dressed
Pour champagne
into a crystal glass
Go to the window
capture the moon
within the liquid
and drink it

Turn off the lights
Go to a mirror
and look at yourself
Walk through your house
Take note of objects
you no longer
wish to touch

Stand naked
in the dark
in front of the window
He will come
Leave time to lock
the door in case you
change your mind

LAUREL ARCHER

Mad Dog

Only mad dogs and Englishmen go out in the midday sun in India, but Ellen's tolerance level is too low for the racket of the bus terminal—Jam fruit! Chai! Garum Chai!—so she waits for the bus outside in the sickly shade of a half-dead cashew tree.

Even the colours of the local temple are washed out by the harsh sun. The fuchsia snakes, saffron vultures, and magenta elephants decorating the blue walls look like two-week-old roadkill. Ellen can't remember why she's taken hundreds of photographs of similar temples throughout her journey. Maybe it's because the Vishnu blue reminds her of the deep, powder-blue paint of Reserve housing back home in Canada. How she longs for the fresh, clean, wilderness. Everything here looks dusty and grey to Ellen. It's like her India eyes have changed colour.

Six months ago she couldn't fill her diary with romantic images fast enough: *white palaces blushing pink under the setting desert sun; fathers and sons silently making their way home through mango jungles and yellow marshes in dugout* canoes; amputees on skateboards doing tricks to Bollywood pop music; and, magnificent women in silk saris, bargaining for gold over the din of business as usual in the market.

It was the utter strangeness she had so loved in the beginning. India was another world, a place where nothing from her culture made sense. She was carried away by India's chaotic, karmic, flow. After travelling in the North, she had written to a friend back home: *Imagine being on a bus on the only road through the Indian Himalayas. The road isn't wide enough for two vehicles coming from opposite directions to pass safely if they are going any significant speed at all. Every corner is blind. There are no guardrails, and you're on the side of the highest mountains in the world. To make it even more interesting, you have a Hindu bus driver. Why would he care if everyone dies in a smash? As long as the accident's not his fault and he's lived a good life, he's on his way to another better one!*

Having the time of my life.

Love, Ellen

P.S. That's why I'm riding on the top of the bus in the photo. If you're sitting inside you don't have chance of surviving a crash where whole kit and caboodle goes over the edge. On top, you might be able to save yourself by jumping off in time!

Ellen's beginning to think she might have smoked too much hash when she'd first arrived in India. How else could she have written such crap? In India, hundreds of people die every second. There's not enough clean water, not enough bathrooms. There's nothing funny or sanitary about people squatting with plastic buckets in hand like kids

at the seashore to shit by the train tracks because there are
no toilets in the slum housing. There's nothing romantic
about an amoeba eating away at your guts because some
idiot didn't wash his hands, Hindu or not. You're the one
that's dead.

Ellen quickly stops her thoughts. If she's not careful, she'll
start sounding like the travellers who never leave The Scene
if they can help it. The Scene is her label for any place in
Asia that travellers congregate in greater numbers than the
locals, usually holy places and beaches. The backpackers
don't mean to wreck anything, but they do in feeding their
desire for cheap food and lodgings, Marlboros, drugs and
beer. The local economies and traditions are destroyed in
the search for the *Feringi* dream. At Kuta, on Bali, young
Indonesian men swagger along the beach with their avail-
ability advertised on their backs in zinc-oxide sunblock.
Fluorescent pink or lime green letters on sun-blackened
skin spell *Fuck me. I'm a gigolo.* In Bangkok, women and
children are kidnapped, never to see the sun again. The
Scene reminds Ellen of the Saigon created by the Vietnam
War. It's awful, scary, but it can be fun, for white people like
her.

She knows she doesn't meet the standards of the "real"
travellers she meets, the kind that learn to speak the lan-
guage fluently, drink the water out of the tap, avoid the sun.
Their eyes view her tan, trinkets and tie-dye as signs of her
membership in the plague of backpackers. But The Scene
has pleasures she just can't forego: wild full moon parties,
good-looking Swedes, french fries. A few American dollars
make life easy, fit for a queen.

Some travellers argue their money is helping the poor. In India, these are most often the travellers that never leave The Scene. It's all they want, or they are too afraid of the "real" India—the India of the Indians, where white people don't have power simply from the colour of their skin like they used to. You only find that off the beaten track, you have to look for it.

The Scene, from Ellen's point of view, is for socializing and resting up from taking the road less travelled. This had been her pattern in all the Asian countries she'd visited so far: travel in the boonies, then stop at The Scene, back to the boonies, and so on. She didn't think she was trying to find herself or save the world, nor was she a tourist wanting a cheap holiday. She'd felt the magic, and was having a good time too, not hurting anyone.

The people Ellen finds hardest to take are the travellers who have "been in India too long," like Digger and Steve, the Aussies she'd hung out with in Goa. She'd been naïve about the attitudes that dominated The Scene until the episode at Chandra's Guesthouse.

Steve and Ellen were playing cards and drinking Arak and Coke at Chandra's bamboo cafe. It was Happy Hour, and they were getting happy. Suddenly Digger showed up, his long hair flying and his John Lennon glasses askew. Steve was surprised Digger was moving so fast. "Hey matey, what's the hurry? Shanti, man. Shanti."

"Somebody nicked me phong!"

Steve stopped dealing. "What?"

"Bloody blackies!"

Ellen scanned the shack for Chandra, hoping he was out

of earshot. The Austrian reading next to her looked up from *Crime and Punishment*. Even the American couple arguing about their next destination stopped for a moment to listen.

"Someone stole your thongs?" Steve asked.

"I was 'aving a sleep and me phongs were sitting outside me door, like always. When I woke up, one of 'em was gone. Nicked, nicked by a goddamned Indian!"

Steve, Ellen, and the onlookers started to laugh. Digger's lisp and Australian accent together were too hilarious. "But, Digger, why would someone steal just one of your thongs?" Ellen couldn't believe he was serious.

Digger had an audience now and continued his rant with even more enthusiasm. "I'll fix 'em buggers. Put a bomb in me Walkman 'at doesn't work, and leave it out on de beach while I'm swimming. Fer sure dey'll come and steal it and de fookin phing will blow 'em to bits. At'll teach 'em."

Everyone roared, waves of hatred displacing the heavy dusk air. It was too much, even for The Scene. Ellen shouted, "Maybe a dog took it, Digger. Did you ever consider that? That a fucking dog might've stolen your *phong!*"

Silence fell like a knife. Ellen jumped up from the rickety table, spilling cards into the sand, and ran out into the night.

She'd headed out the next day without saying goodbye to anyone. She must've eaten something with the amoeba in it shortly after that, while she was on the less-travelled road.

Betel nut juice stains the ground around the tree where Ellen is waiting. She stares at it. It reminds her of the blood. She hopes being in The Scene will erase her memories of lying on a dirt floor spewing her bodily fluids into the cracked earth. Guilt be damned, she needs to join the golden hordes on the beach right now. She will sit at the small tables under the palm trees and drink large, cold beers for 50 cents each and play Kaiser and Bridge. She will speak English, watch the sun set, and have her own bathroom.

If only the bus would come. In a few minutes the shade of the cashew tree will be non-existent, then she'll have to move into the bus terminal, where she'll be swarmed by women selling food and handicrafts. Since she'd contracted amoebic dysentery, her stomach rolls at the sight of the cracked and flattened feet of the working women, the gold in their ears, noses, the death in their eyes. Sure enough, her bowels move, and Ellen closes her eyes, concentrates on not having to go to the public toilet in the bus station.

India is the smell of shit. All the horrible bathrooms she's used haunt her. The first night she was really sick, the cramps were so bad she'd passed out while squatting over the hole in the ground that served as a toilet. She'd come to with her face in the slime on the floor, sicker than a dog, a dying dog.

In the end, she'd saved herself.

It was like she was already dead. Ellen watched herself pull her body from the dirt floor of the hut where she'd collapsed three days before. Against one wall a Sadu was sitting cross-legged in a filthy loincloth chanting and praying for enlightenment. Across from him a British couple were trying to contract AIDS in numerous different ways, their naked limbs entwined grotesquely, streaked with dirt and shadow. Needles glinted in the sunbeams piercing the weave of the palm leaf walls.

It'd been impossible to get a real room in this mountain town full of Indians celebrating Shiva's birthday. She'd been delirious when she'd finally reached the hut under the guidance of a local woman who demanded 30 rupees for taking her there, but she still was coherent enough to feel lucky she had any roof to lie in agony under. Then she'd puked and shit blood until she knew she would die if she didn't get up and get help.

Ellen somehow found the strength to walk the gauntlet of lepers' row back to the main square that was filled with the mad worship of The Destroyer. She was surrounded by beggars, prostitutes, and snake charmers undulating in the heat waves, distracting her from her last-ditch attempt to find a doctor in the midst of the five-day holy festival.

Sweat burned her eyes as she searched the Hindi store signs for a red cross on a white background. She stumbled on, praying she would not collapse under the noon sun in a pile of vomit and blood-streaked shit. She found a clinic, climbed the three concrete steps to the wooden desk where the black telephone and the receptionist sat, and started to cry.

The doctor had been trained in England she was assured. She'd spent three days and three nights lying on a plank with an IV in her arm watching children and pregnant women watch her.

Ellen had sworn she'd go back to Canada as soon as she could travel. But this morning, when she was finally allowed to leave the clinic, she'd caught a bus heading south to the coast. It would've taken her days to get to an international airport—days on a train with a reeking, rocking toilet, days of harassment by sexually frustrated and immature young men, deprived of contact with women their own age. She'd taken the easier path to The Scene, choosing the lesser of two evils.

Ellen's bus arrives just as the shade deserts her. It's a small one, packed with passengers and baggage. She can't bring herself to join the crowd of Indians pushing and shoving to get on top of the bus. She'll have to stand with her pack on in the aisle. At least she'll be in the front where she can get some fresh air from the door. Ellen pays double the price to ride the bus, the white fare, because she is too tired to argue.

It's twenty minutes before the bus departs. The temperature inside makes breathing difficult. The smell of old fruit and garlic sweat is worse. Ellen concentrates on not fainting.

As the bus trundles past fields of faded red earth, a hot breeze dries Ellen's sweaty hair. She daydreams about the cool, blue deeps of the sea. At a village the bus slows. An Indian man says "Kiss me. Kiss me," into her ear.

This is what Ellen hates most about India, the way men on trains and buses leer at her, stalk her, rub up against her whenever they can. She has no mercy anymore. She looks at all of them with eyes that say: Touch me again, and I will kill you. The men understand.

The bus stops. The voice continues, "Kiss me. Kiss me," louder and louder. Ellen feels the passengers' eyes watching to see what she will do. Bile rises. Someone behind her taps her shoulder. She whirls around to confront her harasser with the death look. Startled, an older Indian man in western clothes takes a step back in the aisle. Beside him is a younger man in traditional clothing. They both look at the floor.

"Yes, please, he needs to exit the bus," the older man says apologetically.

Ellen closes her eyes. She moves to one side of the aisle. The young man has been saying, "Excuse me. Excuse me." He just wanted to get off the bus.

While the new passengers get settled, the bus starts up again. For the next forty-five minutes Ellen stands alone in the aisle, ringed by brown eyes. She looks straight ahead, focussing only on the cracks in the windshield, until the bus stops again.

She gets off and crosses to the other side of the road. She needs to catch a bus or a train to the nearest airport.

ELIZABETH RHETT WOODS

Ice Wine

The frozen river winds before us
through the forest, our lantern's
yellow eye reflecting red, while
overhead, Orion stalks the sky,
and a great white owl floats by.

You invade the solstice solitude
like a snowmobile, you can be heard
for miles, misplaced as a moose on ice
you advance, white-on-white treads
congealing, tripping the unwary.

I bury myself in books, in nooks,
in carrels far from Christmas, mute
tongue lingering over your name
is delicious, potent, very dear. No
one here can afford such moonshine,

or the time required to sip it properly,
molecule by silver molecule, like Mercury,
sweet and deadly in the mouth, the message is:
What's yours is yours; what's mine is mine;
what's his, is his.

MAUREEN MCCARTHY

Some Morning

Some morning I might put a coat on,
move along collapsing roads,
stop at gas stations,
phone back to the tenderness that still remains.
Chocolate bar machines are jammed,
cries are spilling over—
the elevator goes down and down, far into the abyss.

At 5, I like to climb the letters of your name,
roll the porch up,
turn on the candle light.
A path appears.
I watch from the warmth of my deep bed
as it floats into my empty suitcase.
I am being called out into the night—
I wonder who I am, and if I'll go.

GEORGE WHIPPLE

First Love

Walking home in the dark
in that in-between time
between night and morning,
my footsteps the only sound
except for the darkness
rustling in the trees;
alone with the moon
sleepwalking to morning,

returning home exhausted
(no doorway so lovely
as the one I just left)
I remember your eyelids
opening like clouds
that unveiled two stars
between each kiss . . . then
closing when we kissed again;

you clarified my sight
then made me blind
to everything but you;
the farther away you are
the closer you seem—
walking home in the dark
in that in-between time
between night and morning.

CORNELIA C. HORNOSTY

The Leap

Her capacity for pleasure,
so limited until now
began to awaken
when the drapes were closed
and she and her lover
felt their smooth mourning
bodies glide, fold out, like
the two white and purple irises
blooming on the balcony, small breezes
fluttering their bright aprons.

Her eyes met the necklace of lapis
lazuli on the dresser
crooning a noiseless blue
inside its silver
oval, her periwinkle socks
on the chair beckoning a voyage, the Gerbera
daisies in a vase smiling their big
red and orange selves, spilling velvet
around the room until too
much happened.

And the cup with
elderberries on it from Bavaria,
the one she coveted, the one
she always tried to use

in the morning for coffee,
hoping no one would find out
how dearly she loved it.

The leap was taking place
from sin and stealth, from grandmother's
Bible reading and sense of wrong
doing and anger about the beer
and laughter
they shared in the kitchen.
Her lover was smiling,
bending close
and she was ready,
eager, her skin glowing,
her hands recognizing
good fortune.

JANICE LORE

Shelling Peas

"How old do you have to be to fall in love?" my son Trevor asks.

The question rises suddenly out of heat waves and clear blue sky, like a mirage right here between us.

I stop shelling peas.

"You only have to be minus nine months," I say. He looks blank and pushes his hair off his forehead. His fingernails are packed with the green flesh of peas.

That's how old he was when I fell in love with him. I always hoped it was mutual.

"Why do you have to fall in love?"

"You don't have to. But it's pretty lonely otherwise."

"But why do you *fall?*"

Ah, the real question, like the left hook after the feint. I don't know. *Because it hurts so much?*

I crack another pod. The bucket is already half empty. I am surprised. I remember how long it took to shell a bucket of peas when I was Trevor's age, even though our mother entertained us by singing and telling stories. Unless our father was there. Then we sat straight up, focused on one pod, then the next one, then the next. Never ate one pea. I wonder how long it seems for Trevor, discussing philosophic questions with his mother.

"How old were you?"

"Depends which time."

Trevor looks blank again, but this time the corner of his mouth pulls impatiently.

"It's not a constant state of affairs," I say. "Well, of affairs, I guess it is, but in run of the mill living—"

Trevor cuts me off. "How old was Grandpa?"

"Grandpa fell in love at the age of—sixteen, I think—and never looked back."

"How did he fall?"

"He looked in the mirror one day, lost his balance and fell headlong through it."

Trevor winces. "Was he cut up?"

"Strangely, he was not. But everyone else was."

Trevor's head comes up and his nose twitches, like a rabbit sniffing something.

"Is that why he calls you a liar?"

⁓

The bucket of peas. It's half empty, it's half full. We could be telling stories. Instead we are falling, into old traps.

FERNANDA VIVEIROS

Lisbon Honeymoon

I wear a rough linen fringe of black scarves round
    my hips
and sway in the courtyard to the music of night-eyed men.
Your whispers of drinking port from the amber cove
    of my throat
don't belong to you, a pale man slipping
    on this country's skin,
and I turn away.

Later, on wall-wrapped lanes clotted with ivy ropes
    and dusky blooms
we step side-by-side back to the hotel. Silent
    women, night-lit and hungry,
linger in the courtyard, your eyes feast in passing.
Your strides become long, impatient to return to
    a cool room,
to a silent meal of ripened pears and sour green wine.

This morning, I dance alone to the pharmacy for
    hand-milled soaps
and medicine while you moan and toss upon the bed,
cursing my native food, the bitter wine, the heavy
    cotton sheets.
A mandolin player outside a café smiles and I
    sing for him,
freeing the words from a wintry cage.

BRIAN BURKE

come & stand by the pool

come & stand by the pool
the night sky in another hemisphere
& the aqua marine light

I'll untie
the strings at your nape
& hip

our initial touch
each other's partial nudity
our skins screaming

with the heat
the apprehension
& après tension

in your last phase of undressing
lying back
you offer me your bikini bottom on extended foot
my mouth full of moss

TERRIE A. HAMAZAKI

Im´potence

School's out and it's another two months until the drizzly overcast days that signal the opening of the Pacific National Exhibition. The endless circles of the fat flies around the dusty light fixture overhead cause Mai, who hangs upside down on the edge of the sofa watching them, to feel a slight dizziness, as if she herself is in uncharted flight. Her long hair sweeps the beige carpet forcing others who wish to cross the room to step over or around its dark pool. Her half-opened book rests face down on her flat chest. Outside, the steady roar of the gas-powered lawnmower is disrupted only by the shrieks of her siblings. Their often-absent father, his eyes shielded from the sun by a baseball cap, walks in a steady pace, pushing the mower in even straight lines.

Mai's mother clucks in silent disapproval at her daughter's languorous pose. She has asked her repeatedly to help with the canning only to be met with heavy sighs that flutter the pages of whatever library book her daughter happens to be in the middle of. Mai lies staring up at the ceiling of the living room, mesmerized by the buzz of the flies. Her mother gives up, shakes her head.

The phone's ringing startles them both. Mai's mom wipes at the sweat on her high forehead, runs her fingers quickly under the cold water tap, dries her hands on her homemade cotton apron. Mai sits up, her attention returning to her book. It is the last of the allotted ten she is allowed, due to the presumed irresponsibility of her age, to borrow from the library. Every week she is a regular visitor, returning home with another collection of carefully selected materials. She eats words with the same hunger that drives her to gulp down her dinner, trying to fill in the blank spaces.

Her mother's conversation, in the Japanese village dialect different from the one she was taught at home, drones in Mai's ear. Only a few minutes pass before the receiver is returned to its holder with an audible bang. Mai starts at the sound, wondering if this was the call her father was expecting. She hesitates before turning another page, her eyes flickering from her mother's taut body back to the text of the magazine that fits neatly inside the open pages of the library book. She stole the *Reader's Digest*-size glossy from the second-hand comic book shop, her pre-adolescent curiosity piquing at the sly titles on the front cover. *Oral Stud Takes on 8 Horny Housewives*, and better, *In Lust With a Lady Cop*. Her hips move against the couch, and a pleasant warmth rises from deep within her. She hears her mother's snort as the phone rings again. This time, to go unanswered.

Mason jars filled with sweet pickled white radishes stand

in neat formation on the kitchen counter. Mai peers over the top of her book, counts fourteen shining jars. She will open them later, stealing a root from this jar, another from that one, her appetite unable to wait for their return upstairs from the basement where they are to be stored until winter. Her mother shakes her head again. Mai's eyes drop. She is not sure if her mother's disapproval is meant for her this time and clutches her magazine-filled book tighter.

The motor outside cuts. A signal to the family that her father has reached the middle of the yard and will now sit on the untrimmed tall grass that circles the trunk of the gnarled plum tree, cracking open a cold beer for his ten minute break. Mai imagines her brother spinning around the stalled mower, his arms held straight out, a plane coming in for a landing. She grins at the sounds of faraway deep belly laughs from her father. He is laughing, Mai guesses, at her sister, who's probably made herself dizzy as she cartwheels around the perimeter of the yard and then collided with her brother in a messy sprawl of pudgy legs and short-sleeve covered arms.

Mai closes her book and slides her body down the length of the sofa. Her mother's slippers slap across the newly-washed linoleum floor, their rhythmic flapping a metronome beat that lulls her into midday slumber. A bloated fly leaves its small group and descends onto her afternoon reading where it washes its face, its plump body covering the first vowel in the book's title of *Bedknobs and Broomsticks*. Her mother stands on tiptoe, peers out the pantry window that looks out onto the yard.

A sudden rapping on the screen door awakens Mai who jerks upright, her book and magazine flipping right side up onto the floor. Her mother rushes to the door, throwing off her apron while glancing over her shoulder.

Again, the strange dialect of her parents' generation rises in its usual angry-sounding tones. But this time, there is a difference. Her mother, normally a gracious host, seems to be arguing with the strange man who pushes past her. He bends over, not to bow in greeting at the women of the household, but to remove his shoes, his stubby fingers yanking at the laces of his footwear. He stands, stares at Mai in surprise as if he's not expecting any children to be inside on such a nice day, and barks commands at her mother. The two females are shocked into stillness. Mai's mother's eyes dart from the man's yelling face to the direction of the back yard. Mai yearns to understand. An uncertain smile appears on her face at the approach of her father.

Now two angry men are yelling at her mother. Mai finds it hard to breathe. Her forbidden magazine is forgotten until the next day when she will retrieve it from under the sofa. There's too much going on. Too many undecipherable words tumbling from all the adults' mouths. Her stomach churns. She doesn't recognize her mother's screaming features. Mai waves her brother away from the living room. He's stopped in the kitchen, their younger sister directly behind him.

In the instant she's turned away from the adults, an explosion.

Her mother is bent over, clutching her belly. Her father pummels her head, her shoulders, any part of her that is exposed and unprotected, with his tightly clenched fists. One, Two. One, Two. His punches connect with their human target, animal sounds carrying each strike. Mai thinks she sees shock and hurt in her mother's eyes when she is finally able to look up at her children. The stranger, the man who set these fast-moving events into action, stands to one side of the room, a slow smirk spreading across his unshaven face. Mai screams and blindly throws herself between her parents who are crashing through the room. She is thrown to the side by her dad, his hands smelling of fresh-cut grass and gasoline, his beer-stinking breath wafting over her head. Her arms spread out wing-like, she shields her brother and sister from the desperate struggles of her mother. She shouts at the stranger for Help! Do something!

But the smiling man walks to the door and welcomes three more adults into Mai's home. From their facial expressions, she understands the older woman in the group is horrified at what she is witnessing, tries to step in between the wrestling couple, but is stopped by the smiling man. The other woman, younger, possibly their daughter, cries into her hands which are clamped tightly against her mouth. Her boyfriend, the only white person in the room, shuts his eyes, turns away, disappoints Mai who is used to watching the heroics of men who look like him on television.

Mai drops to the carpeted floor, her face a distorted mask of pain. Her siblings crouch behind her, their open-mouthed howling reaching nobody but their mother who manages to untangle herself from her husband's fury and clamber over her children to escape through the rear door. She cannot worry about anyone but herself, believing perhaps foolishly, that her husband would not harm them too. Mai struggles to her feet, stands on pins and needles legs to face her father. And empties her heart of any love she ever felt for him.

•‿

This is what she remembers. This is all she knows.

•‿

Five more summers follow this Sunday. Some weekends are quiet, spent visiting other families. The men playing *gaji*, gambling away a small portion of their weekly paycheques, her dad, the only homeowner in the group, throwing away winning cards; the women drinking pots of coffee to stay awake into the early morning hours; the adolescents watching late-night horror movies and stealing sips of warm beer from their fathers' discarded cans. A pleasant visit with friends, then the tired drive back home. But sometimes, her father, drenched in the Hai Karate aftershave he has received each Christmas from his children, his Brylcreem-styled hair gleaming in the moonlight, leaves alone on Saturday night and returns late, drunk and smelling like some other woman.

•‿

Mai suffers through her first crush on her best friend Cheryl, who has no idea that while they are Toni homeperming each other's hair, Mai suppresses the urge to kiss her perfect pink bow-shaped lips. The weekly trips to the library have been replaced with visits to the local 7-Eleven store, where the girls flip through magazines they have no intention of buying, their nervous giggles forming frothy cartoon bubbles over their loose curls. Occasionally, Mai's gaze will flicker to the freely displayed *Playboy* magazines, her acne-scarred cheeks turning amazing shades of red. She will not understand these urges, the need she feels to brush up against her best girlfriend as they paw at pictures of the latest teen heartthrob. Her hunger pangs remain insatiable. They leave the store sucking back blueberry-flavoured crushed ice drinks, the freezing cold giving them both headaches. Later, Mai aims the head of the rubber shower attachment to the spot between her legs, having first adjusted the force and temperature of the water that pulses up her vagina. Her tongue, an undulating turquoise snake, flickers in and out of her chapped lips.

Her mother files for divorce. Returns the kitchen knives to the cutlery drawer. Retrieves them from in between the mattress where she'd kept them. Mai never sees the smiling man again.

Mai licks the solitaire diamond ring that encircles her finger. She will later use margarine to remove its weight from her hand. Her clothes and mismatched cutlery rest in unsealed boxes in the front hallway. Packing tape and a set of his 'n' hers towels lie on top of a neat pile of albums. She waits for her tardy brother and his van. She cannot call him because there is no phone service in the apartment, an unfortunate consequence of her actions last week. Her boyfriend ducked at the last minute to avoid being hit on the head by the flying telephone. Neither could believe the sureness of her aim that time. Both understood it to be the final scene in their three-year courtship. Mai wraps her arms around herself and rocks back and forth on her heels. She makes a promise, tells herself she won't yell at another human being again. The first items her ex moved out were his paintings, saying he didn't trust her not to destroy those too. She whimpers in the fading light, intuitively afraid of the evanescent shadows that have cloaked her insight.

⌣

Mai stares into the crystal ball, seeing nothing. You will go back to school and meet interesting people, the psychic tells her. Mai nods. She has been contemplating a teaching degree in the fall. Your mother will suffer a massive stroke, the psychic continues. But, she will survive. Mai's eyes are wide with fear. The psychic knew about her mom's high blood pressure. Your father. Here, the psychic pauses. I cannot get a reading on him. Why? Her face is full of questions. Mai blushes, looks down at the black velvet-covered table. I haven't talked to my father in thirteen years, she says. The psychic leans back in her chair, holds her hands up, palms facing outward. Your aura is purple, she says. You have a very old soul. Purple is also a sign of royalty. And healing. Mai raises her head.

꜏

I'm just nervous, is what she says to the first woman she sleeps with. Orgasms are overrated anyway, she continues, the low timbre of her voice a raspy sandpaper score from a morning of slogans chanted at full pitch. Their handmade cardboard and wood post signs lean against the bedroom door frame, ready for the next rally, the felt-pen drawn words a plea for the salvation of all womankind. The woman's full breasts sway over Mai's prone body. She draws the contours of Mai's heart-shaped face with the eagle feather she saves for moments like this. Release, she whispers, her breath a hot poultice on Mai's skin. Mai yawns, wanting to withdraw from the older woman's intensity and reaches out an arm to extinguish the candles. She feels a sudden craving for cream-filled cupcakes and pop, falls asleep in an unfamiliar bed smelling of lavender and the sour odour of years of unrequited justice, awakens once, startled by her own cries.

꜏

Mouldy oranges and leftovers from his last dinner hit the bottom of the white kitchen garbage bag. She takes her time going through her father's meager store of belongings, speculating on his final moments, examining each item in his townhouse with the same care that the coroner worked on his slightly decayed body, looking for clues to his premature demise. But soon, the novelty of death's visit having worn thin, she throws his clothes and dishes into boxes for the Salvation Army. She will pause several times in her frenzied clean-up to sit in a crumpled heap in the hollow dining room, holding the last Christmas card she'd given him before he'd left home. Her father, a man who saved nothing.

　

Sometimes, she tries to recall the faces of the family from that sunny June day. But only an outline of the story remains. Her mother shakes her head when asked about that weekend, reminds Mai once more to never interfere in her husband's affairs, urges her to eat more, she's too thin. Mai is still titillated by the cheap erotica she sees at out-of-the-way smoke shops. And when she screams now, it is at the end of her lover's fist, as it thrusts in and out of her body, each stroke marking her pleasure, her freedom.

STEVEN MILLS

Skin to Skin

I

The ragged tearing of her breath into his neck as she bites him hard on the bone of his shoulder. There'll be a small, ugly bruise there tomorrow. He wants her, but he waits, not moving, letting his breath and hers cut at each other, deciding who will move first, who will give in. And finally he sees it, the thing he's been waiting for, moving behind her eyes, looking out with its own eyes.

She drives him backward with her body into the white Kenmore fridge, her mouth hard against his, kissing and biting. The fridge rocks into the wall.

The ice dispenser rattles. She grabs a handful, shoves it against his throat. He sucks in air, the ice shocking skin, then he pushes her away, scooping up his own handful of ice.

She steps back, watches him. He reaches toward her, but she twists, blocks his hand, and behind her the tequila bottle spins, falls, splashing yellow over the counter and the floor and her. She grabs at it, and he reaches up her dress, pulling at her underwear, slapping his handful of ice chips against her skin. She shoves him to the floor and he lies on his back, spilled tequila soaking through his shirt. She pulls off her underwear and stands over him, watching his face.

The thing that he thinks he sees behind her eyes looks down at him, and grins. He tells himself it's only her, that it's just about sex, but there's a part of him that doesn't want to believe it's just her, wants to believe instead that she is alien, other, immutably beyond his reach.

She pulls her dress over her head and throws it on the counter. She drapes her bra over the tequila bottle, then lowers herself onto his hips, slapping away his hands as he reaches for her breasts. She grabs the front of his shirt and rips it open, buttons breaking, then leans down and clamps her teeth onto the skin just above his nipple.

II

"Jesus, I don't remember anything," he says to her as he clinks the spoon around the inside of his mug, the one with the lizard-shaped handle. Clink. Clink. Clink.

"Just drink it," she says.

He avoids her eyes. She doesn't talk much first thing in the morning. He should just stay in bed, he thinks, wait until she's really awake, fully human. But he can't seem to let her alone.

The night comes back in spits and spurts—huge gaps of time lost. Too much tequila, he thinks. Shooting short shots with oranges instead of lemons—much easier on the stomach. They'd raced each other in rounds of eight (that's how many moons he chopped the navel oranges into) biting them out of each others' mouths, licking each others' hands so the salt would stick, then shooting the gold back, cold and fast, gasping at the taste like gasoline in their mouths, and later savouring the brutal flavour, even forgetting about the orange moon afterward.

He slurps the sweet, milky coffee. He prefers herbal tea, barely steeped. But there's no tea left in his cupboards. He forgets to put it on the grocery list. So does she.

She stands, naked, scraping her chair back from the table. He is startled by her nakedness, by the way she wears it like a second skin. It's the aliveness of that skin, the way it slides over her muscles and bones, how it coddles the small pockets of fat on her hips. How it burns his fingers. Suddenly he wishes she would stay home from work. He opens his mouth to say the words, to spit them out into the space he piles up around himself: *Stay with me.* But he snaps his mouth shut just in time, biting the words back.

She refills her coffee mug, her back to him. Her skin shimmies. Lumps blister up on her shoulder blades. Spikes grow from the knobs of her spine. A dark, twisting tail snakes out from between her buttocks.

He stares, panic darting through him like a fish.

She turns, kicks her chair into place and sits back down. Her smooth breasts rest against the edge of the table.

"You're not listening to me," she says, the syllables hitting him like sharp stones and he realizes that she's been talking to him.

.﹀

She rushes around his brown sticky-countered kitchen doing her Tasmanian Devil thing. Keys rattle in her hand.

"I'll be home by five," she says. His home, not hers, he reminds himself, she doesn't live here. She only visits. They hardly ever stay at her place. Mostly she invades his.

⁓

He mops the kitchen floor with Mr. Clean straight from the bottle. Then he writes *oranges* on the empty grocery list on the side of the fridge. And *tequila.*

With a shove, he straightens the fridge. Only ten hours until she'll be back here in his kitchen. Too long. He wants her back in front of him now, tasting her. He shakes his head: but he wants her gone, too, he tells himself, so his life can land again, return to home base. Weeknights she stays here—his house is closer to her office—and lately most weekends. He feels collected—or rather, that he's given himself up, let himself be taken and tagged and caged.

Perhaps it was the way she set her jaw, her mouth partially open, the gap between her front teeth dark, her eyes hard, like basalt.

Perhaps it was that frightening hair of hers, kinky and sticking out, looking like it could eat the hairbrush alive. She tries to tame it in the shower, oppress it with conditioner, but it fights back, twisting and snarling. So dark, only a strand or two of wire-tight grey glinting.

No. It was her eyes that caught him first. Frog-green, and they watched him. She never seemed to close them.

You're a watcher, he'd said to her that first night. I am,

she'd said back. And so he'd looked away, at her chin, her ear, the alarm clock on his bedside table. It was 1:35 a.m. She had to be at work by seven. She bit him and pushed him off her. Her strength was surprising considering how thin she was. But as she turned away to sleep, he'd grabbed her, pulled her back, and in that moment, in the small white light from his fish tank, he first caught sight of the thing that lived behind her eyes, that invaded in order to watch and play and get fucked. He threw her legs apart, but she scuttled backwards, out of his grip. Then she lunged at him, grabbing his hair, pushing him back until he fell, and she jammed herself on top of him, his cock hard up inside her.

He tosses the empty tequila bottle with the others in the recycling bin beside the fridge. Mr. Clean's lemon-freshness burns his nose. He coughs, hand to his mouth, and finds the musty scent of her on his fingers. He smells his other hand. She's there, too, stronger. He closes his eyes, willing her back to him, feeling his face pressed soft against her smooth neck.

III

She's on top of him now, sitting straight up, rocking in a wide, hard circle. Her eyes are closed for once, her head back. He stares at her: the nest of night hair; the small breasts with their too-large toffee nipples; the long, thin neck where her air and blood rush back and forth.

Her face falls toward his, eyes wide, lips loose and soft. He sees it twitching behind her eyes, grinning, taunting him, and suddenly her skin hardens. Rough ridges push outward above her eyes.

An emptiness pierces him like a stake, and in that moment all he can think about is a place he has dreamed: a soft round greenness, open and wild and bright.

His cock goes soft.

She stops, her cold hand on his chest, her soft face close to his. It's gone, the thing he believes he saw.

"What's the matter, lover?" she asks in a voice so tender he begins to weep, and she holds him, rocking more gently now, as he shakes with his private fear.

IV

He strokes the back of her hand as she leans against him on the couch in his living room. A video she'd brought home after work plays across his big-screen TV. He'd stopped paying attention to it; she seemed to be sleeping now.

She fits me well, he thinks, surprising himself, wanting her to never move, to stay leaned against him. Wanting her to need him even in her sleep.

As he strokes her hand, her knuckles bulge. Her fingernails stretch into thick, yellowed claws. A spur grows out of her forearm, and the skin on her arm bubbles and blisters.

He jerks his hands away, waking her, a sob catching in his throat. She stirs, hugs her smooth arm around him, her small thin hand on his hip. She goes back to sleep.

He feeds his fish, scattering the large flakes over the surface of the water.

She comes up behind him, slipping her arms around his waist. Her face presses against his shoulder. "Come have a shower with me," she says, tugging a little. He lets himself be pulled away from the tank.

And as he washes her wild hair, massaging with his fingers, he tries to conjure the thing that lives inside her. He has decided that he is prepared to dismiss it, exile it to the recesses of his imagination from whence it came. He stares hard at the freckled expanse of her back, waiting for the spines and lumps to erupt. Soap suds stream over her skin.

She turns to rinse, her eyes closed, face smooth and open.

.

"You're a goddess," he says to her.

"And you're a liar," she says back, then snorts and pushes herself onto her hands and knees, her nipples above him like miniature stalactites. Her eyes tease, threaten. She kisses him, first on the nose, then the forehead. "Then worship me." She laughs.

And he's between her legs, his tongue stroking her. She grabs his wet hair, holding him. He flicks his tongue-tip back and forth. Faster. He breathes her in, down into his lungs. She smells like mouldy leaves and clam sauce. He tastes cayenne.

"I want you inside me," she breathes.

He shoves her onto her back. She's suddenly passive, and

he drives inside her, closing his eyes so as not to see hers. He can feel her throw her head back, arching. She makes that strangling noise she makes just before she comes, a howl bred with a moan. Hairs flick up at the base of his skull.

She comes hard, panting.

And he can feel its skin: thick, primordial, with rows and rows of tiny, sharp bumps. His eyes open. It grins at him, its kale-green eyes wide with excitement. Then, with a flick of his mind, he banishes it.

She grips his cock inside of her, not letting go, while her body jolts through the orgasm.

Still now, she licks her lips. Slowly, her bright eyes focus on his. He touches her face, his fingers shaking, then lowers himself against her smooth skin, slippery with sweat. He pushes his face into her soft, hot neck, breathes in the smell of her hair, and holds hard onto her, letting himself fall into bright, wild greenness.

JIM CHRISTY

Forever Maria

Just throw my junk out the window,
Baby. It's of no use to me anymore.
None of it is worth a good goddamn
And I can't face coming round. You'd
Just tear a strip off my hide,
Make fun of my haircut
And my twenty-year-old car, this
Second-hand sport coat, our third-
Rate romance. How could
You have ever gotten involved
With the sorry-ass likes of me?

The red suit and yellow wing-
Tip slip-ons? I was never cut out
To be a pimp or an elk.
That glow-in-the-dark Virgin
Of Guadeloupe? All she ever did
Was light the way from your bed
To the shelf that held the booze.
And I never had the nerve
To wear those shirts from Samoa.
Out with the Jim Tully stories, nobody
Cares about them or this shanty Irish
Circus boy, either.

As for the Billie Holiday sides,
Give them the old heave-ho. It
Ain't nobody's business
What you do, as if you ever cared.
Throw it all out the window,
Let the junkman have it, or maybe
You already did let him have it.

Just mail me that bus station photo.
The one where the beautiful young woman
Doesn't look too terribly upset
At being with the future no-good
Worthless son-of-a-bitch who's
Squeezing her close,
There in Saskatoon

She's in profile, smiling up at him
Hoop earring a dangling blur
That's keeping count
Of the time that's running away.
You know the picture, the one
On the back of which, in purple ink,
Is written: Your baby forever,
Maria.

On second thought, throw that
Out the window first of all,
Baby.

YVONNE BLOMER

In Leaving

It's all chaos and echoes:
no green field to wave from in a moment of silence;
no long walk along the river to say goodbye.
It's fireworks, girls in *yukata*, last tea ceremony
last bottle of Kirin or shared sake cup.
We are two bullfrogs on the highway at night
trying to quietly cross the landscape
but the bamboo trembles the night sky,
fireflies light our eyes and we are caught—unsure
        of our path
our eyes become thin, hold us in the moment.
We are foreigners, we take a part of the countrx y
        with us:
the scent of cherry petals, the green tea
        on our tongues.

SANDY SHREVE

Double Wind Blows in Ears

from "T'ai Chi Variations"

This is no place for the doldrums,
though at first your palms are flat,
facing out, calling a halt
to extremes, their opposite seasons.

You reel in summer
from the south Pacific, winter
from Arctic lands,
hold them close, believing

you are capable of taming both
monsoons at once,
that your two lungs can contain
all the howling in the world, transform it

to a warm breeze. You think
you've been turning the wind
into kisses,
but your hands are clenched.

For the first time, you know
how to use your fists, discover

you can strike a blow
at the temple of your enemy.

LINDA ROGERS

Domestic Pleasures

You called the Asian kill stick your
magic wand when you stood naked
in the dark kitchen waving it over
the remains of the day: the breakfast
bananas and oranges, the mangoes you
peeled in bed in the time before sleep,
licking the sticky tropical juice
from your fingers before you played
the mandolin in your devore kimono;
its silk made by worms, the velvet
eaten by insects with acid lips.

It took us so long to come to these
domestic pleasures: velvet, eating
mangoes in bed, permission to murder
anything that gets in the way of
our love, singing *Ma Belle Si Ton
Ame* in falsetto voices while our
children from previous marriages
put their fingers in their ears
and sing louder than us to cover
the terrible sound of fruit flies
exploding in the compost at night.

What attracts men to women who
hurt them and women to outlaws
who commit crimes that condemn
them to die in the electric chair,
where they burn like insects caught
foraging when the lights are out?

Why would the fruit flies fly eating
and singing into your magic wand
if they own the evening? Is it
because we are none of us celestial
navigators; insects, men, women and
children, only a few degrees of
separation between us, compelled
by fear of the unknown to invent
fire every time we find one another
falling, like stars with no place
to land, all alone in the dark?

JACQUELINE BALDWIN

Yak Flatterers

the professor had lived in Tibet
spoke eight languages
was teaching us latin declensions

we were off in teenage dreams
rock and roll, boys, beach parties

we tried to get him talking about travel
divert him from grammar
he would become excited
speak two or three languages at once
without noticing

someone asked him
what future can there be for this country
now occupied by China?

"Ach" he said "very triste"

he told us that in the Himalayas
it is necessary to sing to the yak
appease him
before loading him with all your freight

you hum words
tell him how enchanting he is

how beautiful
in a low voice you describe rhododendrons
blooming in thousands of different shades
in Tibet

your yak-seducing tone
lulls him into complacency
allowing you to creep up on him
invade his life
placate him sufficiently
to get your load
on his back

GEORGE K. ILSLEY

When Parrots Bark

"What good's a parrot who can't even talk?" my father asks again, just to bug me. Dad brought the parrot home only a couple of days ago, as a surprise. The bird's origins were unclear—Dad said the Amazon. The parrot waddled blinking out of the box and onto my hand, his feet scaly-grey and hot.

"I love him," I said loudly, pretending not to notice Mom's face cloud over. "I love him, Dad. I love him."

The parrot is gaudy, blue chested, his head crested with flaming crimson tufts. Brilliant primal colours flicker on his wings and back. When excited the feathers of his crest flare up like exclamation marks, his face flushes, and he barks. He doesn't talk, he barks, and he can growl too, but not convincingly.

"Why is a store open 24 hours called a 7-Eleven?" I ask Dad, as we drive past. We need tampons, birdseed and frozen lasagna. *Three things*, Mom had said. *No need to write it down. Any idiot can remember three simple things.* In the store Dad says, "Look at this bird," handing me a jumbo box of Froot Loops, the toucan crazed with excitement. Dad likes this sweet stuff. Mom refuses to buy it. *Kids' cereal*, she calls it. *Expensive kids' cereal.*

Dad catches me by the shoulder. "We'll just put this in here." He jams a small box of tampons through a slit in the side of the jumbo Froot Loops. "A surprise for your mother."

Fear rises and circles around me, exposing my insides to the world. *He must have made that slit before handing me the box.* I wonder what else he has planned, and check over my shoulder for big round mirrors which see everything. Dad of course has disappeared.

I figure he'll tell Mom I wanted the Froot Loops and Mom will freak out. *I don't know who's worse*, slamming the cupboards and, if she catches your eye, glaring. *That father of yours.* Mom asks why on earth, why go and do something like that? Explanations are never good enough. Dad makes himself scarce until Mom stops asking *Why on earth* and instead says, *Come home.*

I head towards the cash, dragging my feet, feeling slow and heavy and awful, like in that dream where I'm just so stuck and too scared to move.

Again my shoulder is grabbed from behind. This hand is hot and heavy like a thick slab. Turning I see a name tag pinned to light blue fabric. *Myron, Store Manager.*

Myron is huge. *How does he manage to get around without knocking everything over?*

Myron takes the toucan box. His fat fingers fumble into the slit and retrieve the tampons.

"What's this? A surprise in each box." Large light blue Myron is so deadpan I don't know if he's joking or not.

Myron guides me to the check-out, where I pay for the

birdseed and frozen lasagna. All I can think of is arriving home without tampons. But what can I say? *You know the tampons in the Froot Loops? Mom really needs them. So— can we just go ahead and buy them?*

"OK," Myron says. "Tell me why you did that."

I feel totally awful—in fact worse than that. I don't know what to say. I see Dad outside, standing by the car smoking, digging at a rust spot, pretending not to watch me talk to the manager.

Myron hasn't struck me, or yelled. He doesn't even seem pissed off. I feel something pull at me—I really want to tell the truth. (Later, daydreaming doing science homework, I figure this tug of honesty has something to do with gravity because Myron was like so totally gigantic.)

I look at the floor and blurt out—"Dad put them in the box. I didn't know what he was doing, and then, I just didn't know, what to do."

Myron takes a breath, then looks back at me. Like he cares. "That the truth son?"

"Uh-huh."

Myron sighs again and I look up. He knows everything now. I let out the breath I'm holding. "Wha'cha gonna do?" I whisper, my voice shaky.

"What do *you* want to do?"

I don't have a clue but suddenly I tell him. "Why don'cha tell Dad you caught me and you're gonna call the cops. That'll scare him." I look at Myron right in his eyes. *What is he thinking?* I turn away and notice my father dragging the last puff of life out of his butt before flicking it aside and elbowing his way back into the store. "Here he comes."

Myron waves Dad over. Sounding very serious he asks, "This your boy?"

Dad nods, looking at me, all concerned. "Well," Myron says, "he tried to walk out of the store with these"—he waves the tampons in the air and the cashier giggles— "stuck into this box of Froot Loops."

Dad glances at me again. I wait for him to explain to Myron what happened. I smile, watching Myron to see him react as he hears from Dad he was right to trust me.

The slap to my face catches me by surprise. "What are you laughing at?" Dad says, fuming. "This is serious you little shit."

I hold the side of my face with my hand. My head is ringing, spreading outwards, filling my ears, muffling the sound of my own whimpering.

Dad talks to Myron. Can't make out all the words, but stuff like, *Don't worry, take care of this at home. His mother and me'll make him sorry he ever . . .*

His hand on the back of my neck, Dad steers me out of the store and towards our dirty old car. He opens the passenger door and guides me into the seat like he does with Mom when he's being all mushy. When he's all nicey-nice like that Mom and I roll our eyes at each other before Dad gets in on the driver's side. But now, I just stare down at the bag of birdseed and frozen lasagna between my feet. *We need three things. Three simple things.*

Tampons. Last seen sitting there on the counter next to the box of Froot Loops, the small blue box all calm and serious next to the crazy toucan with the rainbow beak. And the cashier giggling, the braces on her teeth a muted gleaming like dirty chrome.

Dad drives without a word. I want to remind him to stop at another store, but don't say anything.

Almost home Dad says, "Now straighten up. And stop blubbering. Before your mother sees you."

This is good news. This means he won't tell Mom. That it's between us. Like it never happened.

Mom was more upset by the lasagna we bought than the tampons we forgot. *Vegetarian* lasagna did not suit her cravings.

"Typical." She takes a big breath and lets it out, sliding the frozen slab into the oven. "No point asking a man to help out. Surprised you remembered a thing." Standing by the stove she reads the ingredients from the lasagna box. "Hydra, hy*dro*-lized vegetable protein." She snorts. "Didn't I say I was hungry enough to eat a horse and chase the rider?"

I shake out some of the new parrot food. The label showed three birds in a row, each looking chipper and eager. Names run through my head as I watch my parrot pick out the larger seeds. Peanut. Sunflower. *Sunny.* Using his beak and thick round black tongue he shells sunflower seeds faster than I can with both hands. "Sunny," I whisper, trying it out. His neck feathers rustle as he turns his head to watch me with one glistening black eye. I want to touch his soft crown, to stroke the precious little feathers on his forehead, but I'm afraid he'll bite. A parrot can't see too close in front of him.

Dad comes back with really expensive tampons from the corner store and throws the bag down on the table. The noise startles the parrot, who squawks like a question, rising higher at the end. "A surprise in every box," Dad says.

Bobbing his head, the parrot yaps frantically, like a chihuahua, *wow wow wow wow wow*, and we all laugh. Mom and Dad and I, all of us laughing. Already the barking parrot is making a difference. He will be a real pet—just like a dog. Maybe I'll give him a dog's name, like Prince. Or Scout. Or Boy.

Sunny Boy. I'll tell him everything, and teach him how to talk. I'll explain it all to him and he can repeat it back to me.

Wow wow wow, Sunny Boy barks. *Wow! Wow! Wow!*

IRENE ROBINSON

After Evie Found the Bird Guide Book

A park employee warns Evie: "Detour. Use the far side of the main path around the lake." In the spring, swans choose to nest on the edge of the path or settle smack in its middle. The path is dangerous. These swans are out to defend their nests. Furthermore, someone has been stealing these eggs.

Evie suggests, "Maybe coyotes or raccoons?"

"They leave bits of shell behind them. This thief is tidy."

Still, daring to steal a swan's egg is hard to figure. One swat from those wings can easily break a grown man's arm. All that for a free egg? Evie, who's well acquainted with going hungry, knows that no homeless person is strong enough to successfully bully a swan.

From a safe distance, she is almost mesmerized while watching the incredible grace of a female swan uncoiling herself. Evie envisions an ancient Egyptian goddess moving with great deliberation. She contradicts herself. What would an ancient Egyptian goddess have to do with a contemporary egg stealer? Evie rereads her newly found bird book. Maybe it mentions enemies like egg stealers. Of course it doesn't, but that night in the half-awake stage, the truth comes to her. This has to be a crime of passion—a mean-minded crime—like jealousy. Then as she falls asleep, a vision of a yoga student spying on the swans fills her mind. The swans, after watching the yoga student trying to emulate their movements and only succeed in tying herself in knots, lost patience. Choosing their bad eggs, and acting in concert, they pelted her. That left the question of who cleaned up the mess but Evie decides to leave that to more sophisticated bird watchers.

A turkey settled down on Evie's balcony. She called the local Audubon Society. "Impossible," they said and refused to talk to her. Neighbourhood birds—crows, pigeons, seagulls and a few starlings—wouldn't tolerate the intruder. They swamped this tiny space. All the bird shit and accompanying stink sent the neighbours crazy. Evie wished her bird book mentioned guano. No, that was what bats did. Either way, a book that was so fussy about birds' "upper tail coverts" should at least acknowledge their droppings.

She decided that if the birds let her out on the balcony long enough, she'd collect their shit and distribute it among her neighbours for fertilizer but this desire to share her largesse didn't translate into anything practical. Instead, she wondered what to do about a stiffly worded letter from the management: "Warning. No Pets Allowed."

Through it all, somehow, the turkey seemed to be getting enough food, looked as though he/she liked living on the twentieth floor but was getting pretty raggedy with all the other birds picking at him/her.

·ᴗ

Evie learns of a free excursion to a recovery centre for birds of prey, and she goes. Who would have thought that some birds needed rehabilitation? One of the women on the tour remarked that a heron had returned near her house for the umpteenth spring.

"Stupidest bird in history," another woman stated.

"Well, the breed must have something on their side," her competitor-for-the-most-bird-knowledge rejoined. "They've survived since dinosaur times."

Evie moves away and watches an almost blind hawk. His breed is brighter, shrewder than herons, but has he lost that advantage now that he can barely see?

The two women approach while discussing an owl with a permanently damaged beak. Evie does not want to know that much about owls with permanently damaged beaks and runs out of the sanctuary into the nearest open field.

Bird sounds, and not melodious ones, fill the air. Two midget-sized red-winged blackbirds chase a great blue heron across the sky. Why doesn't the heron think to turn on this pair and chase *them*? Evie decides that to watch birds and expect to understand anything more about them than what you learn from watching humans is silly.

Evie not only found being poor tough on her spirits, she was fed up with being forced to do things for which she didn't have a talent. As in all the other interviews, the Welfare Worker wants Evie to describe her skills, and she surprises both of them by asking:

"Like a trade?"

The Worker nods.

"I don't have a trade," Evie states. "I have a profession. I am a parrot psychiatrist."

The Worker, who hates her job as much as her claimants hate her, flounders. Where in hell does she slot a "parrot psychiatrist?" Does the computer even have such a category? While she tries to keep her cool, Evie continues.

She doesn't know where the words come from—unconsciously she must have been building this daydream since the day she found the bird guide. She loved every minute of bugging the Welfare Worker.

"It's not so different from being a therapist for humans. Of course, we don't rely much on drugs—they're not really for the birds. Birds need good food, loving attention and a clean place to sleep."

Aware that her lies were going as smoothly as the feathers on an eider's back, Edie warns herself; this could be dangerous. Did she trust herself to know when to quit? She plunges on. Listening to herself tell the end of this story is more liberating than anything she's ever done.

PAMELA PORTER

Rescue Farm

Farm's full of the lost, maltreated, those left
to starve; she rounds up more. Neighbours say
just try to take one home—The last
lady came six times, asked for a different horse
each time, left empty all six times, trailer bouncing.
Billie-Jo's her name, but I didn't come
to take anything home. Still, she talks
like a train on loose tracks, how she yanks
animals out of dead-end lives. Has fourteen
ponies from midway rides, arrived dizzy
and bony. Drives Reserve roads, six months
mud, six months dust, the houses lean
and silent, dogs worn thin. Plucks up mongrels
while the residents, at long house
ceremonies, beat drum and dance.

I bend to scratch their heads, think
it's an improvement, at least—used to be
children who were snatched away. This one's
got a Native sense of play, dry humour,
bit of the prankster the way
he hides in sawdust, pops out his head,
shaking his ears of sawdust snow.
No doubt some child misses him.
This one, regal pure bred, was bred

Too often, held kennel-captive, can't bark.
"Cut out her vocal chords," she informs
on the owners. "She don't take to people now."
I nod, don't say I know how it is
not to have a voice. The dog follows.
I scratch all the places I know dogs love;
she trusts her head on my lap.
Before I know it Billie-Jo comes up
with a sack of dog food. "Never seen
anything like it. She chose *you*."

We wave good-bye to Billie-Jo,
pensive dog and I. The ponies swish their tails,
mouths in their hay, don't notice the two
barkless creatures driving off. Evenings
now, we'll sit together, human and dog
alone in our thoughts, remember the past
and wonder at people who never wanted
what we could say or welcome
our true selves, as though we're somehow broken,
needing to be fixed. Yet since our meeting
bare trees beyond the house windows
astound with blossoms, the sky
broken open to blue. Nights we've agreed
on *bossa nova* over *baroque*, our apple
gleaming silver under the April moon.

JUDY WAPP

The Pachyderms

The floor creaks above her head. They're home. There will be no peace tonight.

The room had seemed perfect the day she saw the For Rent sign in the window of the brownstone, a chilly day, with blustering winds whipping around corners, blowing old newspapers and gum wrappers along the curbs. When Beatrice, the building's caretaker, who smelled of strong soap and wore layers of long skirts, had led her up the creaking stairs to the fifth floor, Simone was breathing heavily and ready to say "No" even before the old woman fumbled with the two locks on the scratched and dented brown metal door.

"Slam hard when you go," Beatrice said in her thick East European accent as she moved heavily away toward the stairs.

The light that spilled on to the wide planks of the floor, lemony in the autumn morning, along with the muffled softness of street sounds below, dissolved any objections to the five-storey climb and Simone whispered "Yes-s-s-s" as she turned slowly around in the middle of the large space.

The perfect peaceful place in which to finish the composition.

Within a week, with the help of friends and Cousin Sally's van, she was moved and settled, even had gauzy curtains on the tall windows and a coat of sunflower yellow paint on the wooden floor. Her keyboard facing the skyline, Simone worked happily, delighted with the pages of notation piling up.

Two weeks later the Pachyderms returned home and Simone learned that the room above hers, a sort of penthouse-shanty, was a dance studio, living space and occasional sparring ring. Of course, Pachyderm was not their real name but what she had decided to call them on the night the couple returned from wherever they'd been, crashing and shouting overhead, while Simone tried to work out some tricky chord progressions and finally had to give up.

And now, of all nights for them to be having one of their foot-stomping arguments, the Pachyderms are threatening to disrupt what precious time remains before rehearsals begin. Not even ear plugs can shield her enough from the shuddering erratic rhythms from above.

Simone takes several deep breaths and wills herself to be calm. After speaking to her tormentors several times in the past weeks, arson has begun to seem the only practical solution except she fears the fire might spread down to her place. Pachwoman and Pachman have reassured her each time that they understand and "will tippytoe around from now on." So far their record time for "tippytoeing" is seventeen minutes.

On the night of the dance classes, Wednesdays, Simone goes to the movies or out to Sally's in Brooklyn. The Pachy

Technique of modern dance involves stomping and bouncing to the throbbing drumbeats of a disco tape, always the same one, music that Simone can only describe as unbearable.

One night she foolishly knocked on their door during a snarling fight about who took out the garbage last. Apparently no one had done it recently. When the door flew open, a rotten onion and mold stink wafted out around the rigid figure of Pachman, a lumbering giant who asked what the hell she wanted. Pachwoman, short and chunky, shoved past him, poking her finger at Simone as she seethed a warning to quit meddling. After the door slammed in her face, Simone noticed several cockroaches scurry along the threshold.

Last week she and Richard, Sally's husband, had tried to lure them out to Long Island with a phone call from Richard, an actor, who pretended to be an artist's agent inviting them to an imaginary address for an audition. They readily agreed to show up that evening, then got into an argument over what costumes to use for which dance number that lasted until four in the morning, the "audition" long forgotten and Simone's evening a complete loss.

And now it is deadline night. The composition must be ready for the printer's by nine the next morning. Simone shrugs into her wool jacket, hat and boots. She needs to get out and away from the racket just to think.

As she turns from locking the door she notices Beatrice mopping the stairs a flight below with what looks like mud from a tin pail. As the old woman steps down from the top step, the mop goes clattering to the next floor down. Beatrice, one hand clutching her chest and the other grabbing for and missing the banister, hurtles after the mop, landing face down, her thick support-hosed legs splayed out behind her on the bottom two steps.

Without even checking, Simone knows Beatrice is dead. She turns back, re-enters her cosy but still shuddering room and picks up the phone.

CATHERINE MCNEIL

contrapuntal listening

i hear the leaves on the hibiscus. they're soon to be
demolished cuz' i was born with one eye and make
a pass at the moon every chance i get. i own her. i
swallow her to decode my own hand.

i look for things underfoot like kiyooka in his
kodakcolapostcards. don't ask me why. i told the
truth about my first/last drunk occurring as a
possibility. of the death of the mother in me. ain't.
woman who can't get over this thing of confluences.
the invisible is coming.

objects are closer than they appear.
butterboycatsmell of turnips at mom & dad's on
sunday. ladeedadeeda. is this inheriting the earth.
my deadcat rebukes me. the sky looks worried.
hasn't the ministry prepared us? i'm giving up the
ghost hoping my insides are in the rightplace as i'm
sitting sideways. in myself.

endomitrial ablation insufficient. "we can leave the
bottom bit of your cervix in." hyster-wrecked me.
i've come undone. i've lost the sun. guess who?
heart outside my skin. st. paul's patient-drop-off.
in-the-out-door.

a walk-in never taking a breath. early morn' of
seagulls wings & fractal sealight. bebop to
pitterpantherpatter by the duke. dream all day long.
shall i see my captain as i cross the bar? people
wanting to leave so soon while dr. van belzin busy
storing the organs of dead children.

& everyone is on psychotropics. seagull squall. body
sleeps in second position. corn moon between my legs.
fecal matter from waterfowl leeching into Georgia
Strait and i don't recognise my hands. we're all
canaries in the mine dying. mere throw aways. if i
could buy silence. in the west end. clamber out of the
well worn dip in my mattress.

this work through which my whole life sings. may i
have your eyes? listen to Chopin's Melisma with your
ear while fluid jingles my anvil. taste the beast within
your beauty for each day my alien grows 600%

as the bus coughs i forget my narrative. as things
underfoot are less reliable. as objects loom larger than
& not what they appear. as my eye askew, iris-blue,
pupil-white, as the other, pupil-blue, iris-white as one
is in the chimney, as the other in the pot.

an old load, an old year. i'll never hear a mother
ship rumble in forgotten places. we could flatstone up
the lazy river. open on the cottage of the thin past
while the cat's ears grey and i think about dyeing
his fur. cover my head. evanesce.

PEGGY HERRING

Flesh Surrendered

The surgeon is behind his desk. It is a huge expanse, a desert of arborite. Janet gazes across this distance. It's impossibly clean.

She never thought she'd come to this point in her life, when she would care enough to let someone cut open her face. But she supposes she is here simply because she is vain and weak. Vanity, vanity thy name is Janet and yes, she is a woman, but she doesn't know if that's got anything to do with it.

Like a desert flower, a jar of pens and pencils appears. She studies the colours, the lids, the leads. Sharp blooms. Will they wilt in the evening? Should she pluck them now, put them in sugared water, try to preserve what is left of their gorgeousness?

The surgeon draws an oval on his desk with his finger. But he looks into her eyes. The eyes whose wrinkles have propelled her here. He looks into her eyes, but not really into them. Around them. His eyes are a machine scanning the delicate skin. We cut here, he says. Just a little slice. His fingers move on the desk top. And then we pull the slack skin up here, he goes on, gestures on the desk. And we attach it here.

She considers the slice. As if her face is bread. Or salami. What happens to the piece he cuts out? Is it prepared in sauce with herbs? Served up to the goddess who determines whose cosmetic surgery will be successful and who will end up looking like a victim from the burn unit, a stern expression planted onto her face, with tiny white scars that never tan?

She wants that piece of flesh. It will not be sacrificed to the goddess, she doesn't want it to go into the hospital incinerator, or a great green garbage bin with used bits of gauze and bandages and body parts from other people. She wants her skin.

⌐

Her father, Ben, shows her how to stack firewood. Row by row, on wooden pallets, just outside the basement door.

"Like this." Ben lays the splits side by side, no breathing room between. Each piece precision cut with his chainsaw, then split down the grain with his axe, the perfect size for the woodstove every time.

"Do it right. Once the snow starts flyin' I don't want to be restackin' the woodpile."

He returns to the chainsaw. She starts pulling the splits from a mounded heap he has already created and stacks them on top of the foundation he has already laid. She smacks the ends that stick out with the palm of her hand to make them even. All this arranging gives her slivers.

The pile grows. The chainsaw shrieks. Belches burnt oil and gas. The stench is raw. As if something has been born in the wrong season.

The pile is nearly as tall as she is. She must lift the splits above her head now. It takes her whole body weight to smack the pieces into place.

With both fists, she pounds at the ends of the wood.

"Janet! Watch out!" Ben shouts. She looks his way. One ear registers a hollow rumble, the other hears the dual wail of the chainsaw and a human howl that cuts the air like lightning.

Blood spurts. Her father's finger flies off his hand. The chainsaw falls.

This picture freezes as the falling wood splits strike her back. The pile she has so carefully arranged knocks her down, tumbles on top of her, then buries her.

Janet has one thought before she is swallowed by unconsciousness: she will ask her father if she can have his bloody finger.

⁌

She will dry her skin on a cedar rail rack beside the beach. She will build a scarecrow, adorn it with old silk scarves and festoons of pantyhose, to keep the birds away. Prevent them from picking at her flesh, soaring into the sky and attacking one another to get at it.

When her flesh is thoroughly dry, she will attach it to a long golden chain. Let it hang between her breasts. And when she shares cocktails with acquaintances and they say, oh, how interesting, where did you get it? She will tell them, it comes from me. It is Me.

Are you sure, the surgeon asks. The sand shifts on his desert desk. The dunes are her wrinkles, their valleys her dark circles. Go ahead, she says, I understand. But you need to be aware of the risks, he says.

She already knows about risks. And accidents.

At the cocktail party she will speak of Dolly the Sheep. The human genome project. Stem cell research. What they do in labs these days. How that dried flesh can be coaxed to grow in a petrie dish, cell by cell, into another woman, a woman who looks, acts and thinks like her. Is Her.

Book an appointment with the receptionist, the surgeon says. She'll give you instructions. And she nods, smiles. But not broadly. She wants to hide her imperfect face.

⌒

"Ray has a red Camaro." Janet is halfway through her hot chocolate.

"Really." Ben has taken her to a movie, then for a hot drink. This is their weekly meeting, as dictated by the custody agreement.

"He has one hundred and eighty-seven records."

"No."

Ben is not impressed, so Janet tries another subject. The movie they have just seen. It was about a robot, about The Future. She loves the dark, the mystery, being swallowed by the soundtrack. She loves the fantasy.

Ben interrupts. "You know Janet, if he ain't good to you, just let your old man know, eh?"

She is not sure what this has to do with the movie, but has an overwhelming sense that she must repair something.

"Dad, he's really nice. He's getting me a new bike."

"What's wrong with your old one?"

"Nothing." She plays with her paper cup. Shakes it side to side, creates strange currents in the hot chocolate.

"Then whaddya need a new one for? Why didn't you tell me you wanted a new bike? I could've got you a bike."

"Dad, it's okay. He knows someone. A friend or something. He works at Russ Hay's." They are watching the whirlpool in her cup. "Anyway, I don't really want it." She shrugs. "But if it'll make Mom happy . . ."

The hot chocolate splashes over the rim. She jumps and then freezes, waits for Ben's reaction.

He almost manages to conceal his fury behind a forced laugh. He struggles to hand her a paper napkin. Still clumsy. He's not used to functioning without his index finger yet.

"You know I had a blue Mustang." He tosses the napkin on top of the spill. The wetness grows, spreads into the paper.

·ﾉ

The surgery instructions are on recycled paper. She reads them in the bathtub. Lists of numbered items, neatly arranged under headlines, stacked in columns, aligned so as to make them clear. Transparent.

Hematoma. Necrosis. Wound dehiscence. Ischemia. Janet cannot absorb the medical terminology. Her eyes lead her back to words she does understand. Abnormal scars. Normal nerve injury. Depression. The description of risks goes on for five pages.

And then at the bottom of the last page: "Warning: Although every attempt has been made to provide a reasonable amount of information, it is not possible to anticipate every potential outcome."

She steps out of the warm water, emerges from her white porcelain chrysalis. Before she can wrap herself in a towel, her reflection appears in the mirror. Water spider. May fly. Wet streams run down her arms and legs, over her sagging breasts, her rounded belly, down, down, they flow and disappear.

Her eyes meet her eyes. Thoughts of problems, outcomes and risk evaporate. Who is that aging woman? She doesn't know. But understands what she wants.

﹏

Ben strains to lift the cardboard box onto the tailgate. He pushes it into the bed of the pick-up, where it comes to rest against a red suitcase.

"Watcha got in there anyway?"

"Books." Janet sets down another box.

"Whaddya need so many books for? Don't they have a library at that university?" He pushes the box into place.

"That's it, except for my bike." She heads for the garage, reappears, a gentle tick-tick-tick of the bike's gear mechanism announcing her return.

"What's wrong with your bike?" Ben grabs the frame.

"Nothing." She pulls the bike back.

"Then what's that noise?"

"What noise?" He kneels, pokes his middle finger into the chain and greasy gears. His middle finger which now plays the role of an index finger.

"That ticking. I can fix it."

"Dad, that's nothing. That's normal. That's the way bikes sound now."

He stops poking. Like a fan, his finger, hand and arm fold back into his body.

"I have to go and say goodbye." She waits. "Are you coming?"

He looks at his hands, smeared with black grease. Swallows. His Adam's apple dances in his thin neck. His jaw twitches. "I'm not meetin' anyone with this shit on me."

"Nobody cares about that. Come in. Please. Mom wants to see you. Ray would like to meet you."

But he has turned back to the truck. He slams the tail-gate with more force than is necessary. Full metal stop.

"No, you go on and do what you have to. And hurry up. We're late." He brushes dust from the truck.

⌁

Janet outlines her eyelids with a green pencil. She is an artist, a creator, draws highlights and masks shadows. She marks a trail on the surface of her skin. Then smudges it with her finger.

She leans in to the mirror to take a closer look. A green

path. To where? Lines that fan out from the corners of her eyes, intersecting, overlapping. A road map of confusion. The skin does not spring back into position as it once did.

But why not? She's done everything right. Knows the regimes by heart. Creams and masks, plenty of water, adequate sleep, cucumber slices or tea bags to reduce puffiness. She never failed to pat dry the way she was taught.

But her skin has a will of its own. Does not listen to her. No longer responds to anything she does.

The surgeon's knife will halt this wilfulness. Re-establish the natural order. The surgery is justice restored. A way to seize back what is rightfully hers.

She caps the pencil. Places it in a jar on the vanity with the other pencils, tubes, brushes and sponges on sticks.

⁓

Ray turns the hamburgers before an audience of family. He tosses patties in the air. They usually land back on the grill. But he misses one and the dog scampers over and cleans up the mess.

Janet laughs. "Come on, Burger Master! Don't let us down." She laughs and laughs, it's a party, she laughs, her words harder to control as she drinks another daiquiri. The aunts, uncles and cousins who have come to see her, on her annual family vacation, are blurry.

"You worry too much. Like your mother." Ray splashes beer onto the grill. Flames erupt, then subside. "Everyone gets a fair share, mutt included. Anyway, why should you care? I thought you never touched this stuff."

"True. But I have a policy: never stand between a man and his poison."

Ray makes the sign of the cross over the barbeque. "Oh Jesus, save me from another food evangelist!"

Janet laughs. "It's good to be home."

"And we're glad to have you back." Ray pulls her close. "But don't get too comfortable."

She laughs some more. This banter feels like old flannel.

"Did you see my new camera? State of the art." He lets her go. Sips his beer.

She drains her glass. "I'm going to get another drink."

She is alone in the kitchen. The sound of family chatter is distant, the alcohol dragging it further away. She is at the end of a tunnel listening to their noises. She takes a pitcher from the fridge and pours another daiquiri.

Ray is behind her. She jumps a little.

"I have never understood why a girl like you doesn't have a bunch of boyfriends hanging around."

Janet takes a drink and laughs. "I'm way too busy for that. You know I love my work too much. Anyway, they'd have to find their way around all your new gadgets just to get to me."

He laughs. "You got a problem with my gadgets?"

"They're your gadgets. You got a problem with them?"

"Well . . ." he says, drawing out the word. "No." They both laugh. And laugh.

Janet has spilled some of her drink on the counter. She wipes it away with her hand.

"Ooops," he says. Snatches up her hand. Pulls her toward him. Kisses her.

There is an instant, so small it nearly escapes notice,

when Janet thinks "no." But it is knocked aside by insistent desire. She kisses him back. Hard and long.

The kiss is over. Sobriety becomes a brick that strikes Janet on the back of her head. She pushes him away.

"Don't you ever do that again," she whispers.

He laughs. Raises his eyebrows. "Are you sure?"

The linoleum shifts. Voices merge, grow louder, until she cannot stand the shouting. She runs for the bathroom, ready to vomit. Kneels before the toilet.

Her body defies her for the second time that night.

･ﾞ

The atmosphere in the waiting room is hushed, like church or school. Some people read tattered magazines with missing pages. Others stare into or through the walls and ceiling. Nobody talks.

A small boy kicks his sandals on and off. Sips from a can of Dr. Pepper. It is not evident if he is a patient, or waiting for someone.

Janet reads a brochure. The Phases of Healing. There are three: inflammatory, fibrosis and maturation. Words like swelling, discomfort and pressure creep over the page, burrow under her skin, begin to nest.

The surgery will begin anytime. She waits to be called.

"In the maturation phase of healing, the patient will notice a change as the skin texture softens and normalizes," she reads. "Swelling will abate. Irritation will fade, as the final result of the surgery is unveiled."

This may be true for the skin on her face, but it will not

be true for the skin she will wear around her neck.

In its maturation phase, this piece of flesh will shrivel up, then grow tough. As blood inside dries, it will yellow. Its edges will be jagged where the scalpel has cut. And it will float, take on a quality of infinite weightlessness. Grounded only by a gold chain, captured between her breasts.

"Janet Springer?" The nurse spots Janet. "Follow me please."

And the nurse leads the way down the corridor, passes through heavy metal doors, the kind with tiny windows through which you cannot see.

LORANNE BROWN

Cycles of Loss

The phone rings on my desk. I answer it automatically:
"Justice Riordan," and wince. *You know you're getting senile
when your professional persona answers your home phone
on a Saturday.*

"Dad, it's me."

"Who is this?" I bark, delighted. "No one calls me
'Dad.'"

I hear his hesitation. "It's right here on my birth certifi-
cate. 'James Sullivan Riordan, Senior: father.' That's you,
isn't it?" He pauses. "Was it so terrible being my father?"
His voice breaks just a little, betraying his vulnerability. I
regret my flip answer.

"Jamie. Son." Christ, he needs a father once in thirty
years and catches me acting the fool! "Being your father was
my favourite role. *You* chose not to call me 'Dad.' Was it so
terrible being my kid?"

That's it, you old idiot. Shift the guilt; make this about
you. Damn it, I'm failing him. It'll be my own fault if he
hangs up.

Desperate, I ask, "What's with all this paternal philoso-phizing? Should we start this conversation again? How's the practice? Still defending the 'criminal elephants'?" *Wrong!* Christ. That's what Gage used to say. I change tone— "What's the matter, son?"—and immediately imagine the worst.

"Mariah's pregnant, Jimmy."

"Oh." Relief. Surprise. Delight. Dismay. Pick a card, any card. "How is she?"

"Incandescent."

Yes, I can picture my daughter-in-law, pregnant again after—what? fifteen years? "How far along?"

"Days. Hours." He snorts. "The tests are much more refined than when Gage was born. Now they can measure the intensity of the gleam in your eye and determine from her basal temperature and the phase of the moon whether conception will occur. And, if so, what sex the zygote will be. Man," he runs out of steam, "I feel so old."

"You might as well be a hundred; you're not getting any younger, Jamie. Is that what's bugging you? You don't sound delighted."

"I'm so tired, Dad!" Twice in one day he's called me that. I close my eyes to press it into aural memory. "I look at all the energy I expended on Gage and it's daunting. I don't think I have that much to give any more."

Christ; poor lad. I feel the pain in his voice, feel my own heart seize. *He needs wisdom, Judge Riordan!* I clear my throat gently, measure my words with care. "It's not the weight of giving that you feel, Jamie. It's the weight of loss. You don't have the strength to *lose* that much again."

The rightness of these words is small comfort weighed in the balance against my son's sorrow. He breaks down, thousands of miles away. "How many times can you lose the same child—" he asks, "over and over and over again?"

The only consolation I can offer is my silence while he weeps long distance.

I honk into my hanky. "He was your son, Jamie. You can't *not* feel the way you do. He was your son."

"You forget," he croaks. "He *wasn't*."

I harumph into the silence on the line. "You're right, James. I for*get*." I drop the sympathetic paternal note: *Mister* Justice James Sullivan Riordan intones from the bench.

"That is my supreme compliment to you, James, as my son; to you as a fine man; to your demonstrated ability as a father. When you took your mother and me aside after Gage was born . . ."

I ignore his moan of discomfort.

". . . you were so fierce and determined that it should be so, Jamie, we dared not question your edict! I had my doubts at first that you had the courage to pull it off, because I wasn't sure that *I* might, under similar circumstances."

"Dad."

I charge ahead. "But watching you with Gage over the years, son: I for*got*. I'd say to Sonja, 'Look at that—Gage is so like Jamie at that age.' Your mother would smile that secret little smile and only then—only then—would I remember. It took my breath away, James."

Silence. Have I gone too far? Or not far enough?

"I was so proud of you. Look at my fine, brave son, I'd think. See what a *good* man he's grown up to be! So strong he can move mountains with his love." I cough for effect. "Yes, Jamie. I forgot. And that was solely your doing. You were a good father."

"So were you, Dad."

His words are reluctant, yet I am convinced he's sincere. My heart fills unaccountably. Surely I'm too old to be affirmed by him, after all this time. Surely the need for this sort of recognition fades, like potency, with age.

And yet, "I can't tell you," I start, "how strange and wonderful it is to hear you call me 'Dad.' It's a silly little thing, Jamie, but it means a lot. Forgive me for being a maudlin old fool."

"I never really let you be my father, did I?" He sounds surprised. "When did I stop calling you 'Dad?'"

"You were about ten. One day I was Dad, and the next I was demoted to Jimmy." I ruminate on this briefly. "No, that's not quite right. It's not that I was demoted; it's as if you were elevated to grown-up. Equal. Peer. But you wouldn't let me be your dad. It killed your mother that you wouldn't let her in as 'Mom' either. 'Sonja and Jimmy,' Jamie's house mates. Or *Sully's* house mates—that's about the time you named yourself 'Sully.' You insisted we call you Sully. It was impossible for us. But you convinced everyone else."

"And now Mariah's the only one who calls me 'Sully.'"

"And you're the only one who calls me 'Dad.'" My voice is much too husky.

"We'll talk soon." And he's gone.

I hang up the phone and rest my head in my hands. Shit.

I can't judge the success of this address; the jury's out. Yet, I feel it hasn't gone entirely wrong. I've done worse. And if the searing pain in my gut is any indication, Jamie's managed to transfer some of his tension to me. If his heart is lighter, then I'm glad of the pain. But it might go easier on my ulcer if I off-load a portion onto my wife. I leave the den, shuffle down the hall into the family room.

Sonja looks up from the newspaper. "Who was that on the phone?"

"Jamie." I forestall her 'why couldn't I speak, too?' face. "He wanted to speak to his father."

"The milkman doesn't deliver on Saturdays," she teases.

I nod as if I haven't heard, sit next to her on the couch. "He even called me 'Dad.'"

"Now I *am* jealous!" She strokes my knee fondly.

"Mariah's pregnant."

"Oh!" Such an expressive syllable—Sonja's voice carries all the variables my own did, moments ago.

"The prospect of having another child has torn the scab off Gage's death. He's bleeding all over again."

Sonja puts her head against my shoulder. "My poor, poor boy! I wish we could help somehow. But he's always been so," she searches for words, "so *detached*. So self-sufficient. Even when Gage died, he pushed away our help. As if he was born fully grown up, not needing parents."

Her words open little rabbit holes for me, like clues left in a dream. I try to follow the trail. "And yet, he used to call his father-in-law 'Dad.' Not even a blood relation! I don't have to tell you how jealous that sometimes made me feel."

"Poor Jim." She squeezes my hand.

"The way he sees it, I pushed *him* away. As if I'd for*bid*-den him to call me Dad." I examine my conscience. "I suppose I eventually started referring to myself as 'Jimmy' as a kind of self-defence, as if it had been my own idea, as if I didn't *like* being called Dad. 'Was it so terrible being my father?' he asked me. I haven't heard that voice in thirty years."

I look into my wife's welling eyes, feel the stinging in my own. "Sonja." I can hardly speak for the pain. "Was it me? Didn't I love him well enough?"

My tiny fair wife holds me in her arms. When did she segue from white-blonde to just plain white? A difference so subtle it must have happened almost invisibly, like leaf-change in the fall. One day you wake up to the obvious change in season, the evidence of decline.

"Well," she says sensibly, taking charge. "Can you remember the first time he called you by your name? Or me by mine?"

I press my fingers to my eyes in order to make more intimate contact with my brain. It was almost thirty years ago, after all! Had I let it go without comment as a passing phase? Or had the pattern already become established before I noticed it? Listen. Listen.

I hear his voice, repeat his words: "'Sonja's dead, isn't she.'"

"What?!"

"I'm sorry, sweetheart." I kiss her forehead hurriedly. "I can't swear it was the first time, but it was *a* time."

"*When?*"

I think. "After the last miscarriage." She'd called me before she called the ambulance. "Make sure you get home before Jamie does," she'd said, "so you can clean the bathroom." She felt so bad about the first miscarriage, at the circus, when Jamie was four. All that blood—and the boy coming off the merry-go-round to find her being carted away on a gurney. "He beat me home from school that day," I say.

Her face is pale; I swear new lines have appeared in the last few moments. "Jim. I made you promise!"

"There wasn't enough time! I was downtown; they'd had a fire drill at school." How can I sound so defensive about a thirty-year-old incident? "He beat me home."

I try to reconstruct my movements that day—no mean feat, since I can hardly tell the difference anymore between my home and my office. But I stand accused of failing to keep a promise to my wife.

"I came in the door." I remember that clearly. "I called his name and he answered from his room. I checked the bathroom on my way."

"And?" she tugs at my sleeve.

"And I went into his room." I offer open palms, *fait accompli*, and a shrug.

"You didn't clean the bathroom?" Sonja's voice is uncharacteristically harsh.

"I told you," I repeat patiently. "I *checked* the bathroom. There was a minute quantity of blood up under the rim of the toilet, so I flushed it. And went into Jamie's room."

She pinches the bridge of her nose. "Why didn't you tell me?"

"Well, *darling*," I say. "You've always been so fastidious, I just assumed that this minute—and I mean *minute*—quantity

of blood was your usual hyperbole, your exaggerated and anal
retentive definition of *filth*. I felt that I'd successfully disposed
of the evidence!"

When Sonja opens her icy blue eyes I am instantly
stricken with shame. "Jimmy. When I left it, that bathroom
was an abattoir." Her voice falls to an accusing whisper.
"There was blood everywhere. *Your son* must have cleaned
it up."

Jesus God.

—*Sonja's dead isn't she.*

—No, Jamie. She lost the baby; she's in the hospital but
she's going to be just fine.

—*I suppose I'll have to stay with Mormor and Morfar for
a few days. Again.*

—I'm afraid so, son.

—*I asked Morfar last time, how come Sonja keeps trying
to have babies? Isn't one child enough? And he said, no,
Yamie, vun child iss never enough.*

—Your grandfather is a *farmer*, Jamie! Farmers need lots
of children.

I'd put my arm around him, but he shrugged it off, drew
away. And—I see it clearly—never called me Daddy again.

Sonja leans against my shoulder as if deflated of all
strength. "I lost four babies, Jimmy! And then I lost my son."

Jamie. Like a polite and helpful boarder all those years. So
grown up. So mature. Even his recklessness as a teenager
was just a way of refusing childish limits. He was testing the
range of his capabilities. Sparring wits with me like an equal,
debating. Where other boys would be wrestling with their
dads or out pummeling each other with hockey sticks, he

would sit with us by the hour, engaged in earnest conversation. Only Jamie himself was surprised when he decided to follow me into law.

"Christ—he's been cleaning up other people's bloody messes all his life!" I explode. Accepting Gage as his own; picking up the pieces of their lives after Mariah tried to kill herself. Losing Gage. I close my eyes against my son's sorrow. "Even criminal law is nothing but cleaning up one bloody fucking mess after another."

My son abandoned his childhood thirty years ago. Because we—*I*—failed to protect him. Insulated himself against loss—by abandoning us.

"What can we do?" Sonja's face is wreathed in pain. "God! I feel like I've lost him all over again."

These cycles of loss—losing the same child over and over again—are inevitable. Not all the losses are as final as death, but all of them are real. Ripping the scab off a barely clotted wound three years, thirty years, after the fact—it makes no difference. It never hurts less.

How many times can you lose the same child, Jamie? How many opportunities do you have to get him back?

I pick up the phone, dial eleven digits.

"Hello, son. It's Dad."

PATRICK LANE

The Death-Watcher

That little boy I told you about died yesterday.
At the end I watched the tumour grow. It was
like a brother or mother, something alive
that owned a part of him. His flesh flailed.
Is that how you say it? His hands and arms
were flails that tried to beat his body back to
where it began. It was like watching a thing
that doesn't know how to arrive
at the earth again, someone so young
he hadn't learned to remember. A *portal*
is what we call it, we who sit with the dying
and make ease the world the blood knows,
helpless at seeing what is made alive go dead,
but easing anyway with words and touch.
I am one who watches for the doorway into death.
Finding the portal is easy for the old. They know
the way. They want that egress, the light
that shines them into night. But the little ones,
this boy? He wanted less. He didn't know how
and so he beat the thin air with fists.
I remember watching women
beat the first rice under the heavy sun of China.
They were the breathing of the earth, the unity
bodies know when they work in the music
of their flesh. The grain fell away with all

the promise grain has for spring and earth.
Promise, you could say. The song of women
in the sun is birth no matter what they do
to hide the love they have. But this boy, this boy—
there was no holding him down, unless we
bound him, and who would bind a child so near
to death? I think it's what we must allow.
What does bruising or a broken bone mean
to a child who wears upon his face his face
grown out of him? The tumour never tired.
You are a poet who can find the still moment.
I know that of you, have read your work.
Find it for me here if you can. We, the death-
watchers, have need of words we can use
for the other boys to come. And they will come.
Each night I lay on my bed and waited for the call
that would lift me to his death. And so it came,
and the boy died flailing. I thought of a bird,
some origami thing I might build that would
take the body of the child, be a kind of boat
with wings that might bear such pain away.
The portal is the place he looked for.
I saw him searching with my eyes
while the mother wailed and the father sat still
as old wood in the corner, something once alive
that bears upon its skin the scars
steel makes when it scrolls and arabesques
a pattern for the blind. You bind in death
what you cannot bind in life. He flailed, just
as the women beat what they had grown

back into seeds for the harvest yet to come.
They go on because they must. Oh, I know,
that's easy to say. The hours went by.
I'd never seen a tumour grow alive so fast.
Then it was over and we cleaned and bound him.
Strange how I thought when I was binding him of you.
Write me a poem. Tell me what you know
that I might read it out to those
whose boys must die. And the portal, yes,
he found it at the end. They all do, you and me
and everyone. What we think is hidden lies
in the open for us to see. There are nights
when what I am is a withering. There are nights
when I stare right through myself and find
beyond my bones a dying all my own.
That's the stillness I think you know
and that's what your poem must do.
It must do what it can for me.

CONTRIBUTOR NOTES

LAUREL ARCHER, who lives in the Comox Valley on Vancouver Island, works part-time as a wilderness guide and canoe, kayak and outdoor leadership instructor. She has published in magazines such as *Chatelaine, Explore, Paddler* and *Kanawa*. She is the author of *Northern Saskatchewan Canoe Trips: A Guide to 15 Wilderness Rivers*.

LUANNE ARMSTRONG has published three children's books and two collections of poetry as well as four novels, of which the latest is *The Bone House*. She has an MFA in Creative Writing from UBC in Vancouver where she is now completing her PhD. She is the managing editor of Hodgepog Books, a publisher of literary and children's books.

JACQUELINE BALDWIN, the author of *Threadbare Like Lace*, has given more than 200 readings. She lives in Prince George and is the designer and facilitator of a workshop on "the healing art of story."

YVONNE BLOMER's work has appeared in *Room of One's Own, Mocambo Nights, Amethyst Review* and *The Fiddlehead* as well as English-language magazines in Japan. She lives in Victoria.

KATE BRAID worked as a carpenter for 15 years. Her latest poetry collection is *Inward to the Bones: Georgia O'Keeffe's Journey with Emily Carr*. She lives in Burnaby.

LORANNE BROWN's first novel, *The Handless Maiden*, was nominated for a BC Book Award in 1999, the Chapters/Books in Canada First Novel Award in 1999, and the International IMPAC Dublin Literary Award in 2000. She teaches writing and communications at Trinity Western University in Langley.

BRIAN BURKE of Vancouver has taught at various universities and colleges and is himself a graduate of the writing programs at both York University and the University of British Columbia.

JIM CHRISTY of Gibsons is a poet and fiction writer as well as a visual artist. He has published numerous books and had several one-person shows; he also travels widely. His most recent book is the story collection *Tight Like That*.

Shannon Cowan's first novel, *Leaving Winter,* was published in 2000. She also writes short fiction, and her stories earned her first place in the Eden Mills Literary Competition and a nomination for the CBC Literary Prize. She lives in Sointula on Malcolm Island off the east coast of Vancouver Island.

Linda Lee Crosfield has been published in *Room of One's Own, Horsefly* and *WordWorks* as well as in magazines in the US and New Zealand. She was a fiction delegate to otherwords 2002. She lives in Ootischenia.

Lorna Crozier, who teaches writing at the University of Victoria, is the author of *Inventing the Hawk,* which received all three of Canada's national poetry awards: the Governor General's Award, the Pat Lowther Award and the Canadian Authors' Association Award.

Laura J. Cutler is the author of the short story collections *Out of Her Backpack* (2001) and *Jumping Off* (2003). She is temporarily exiled in Calgary.

Jan DeGrass of Gibsons has been a freelance writer and editor for 20 years, contributing to the *Globe and Mail,* the *Vancouver Sun,* the *Province, Canadian Living, Chatelaine, Wine Tidings* and *Room of One's Own.*

Les Desfosses of Vancouver is a lawyer who retired early and has published short fiction in *Slice of Life, Whetstone* and *Wascana Review.*

Lorne Dufour, who lives in McLeese Lake, is the author of two poetry collections, *Sit on Wishes* and *Starting from Promise.*

Alexander Forbes teaches at the University College of the Cariboo in Kamloops. His poems have most recently been published in *Canadian Literature* and *Sentences and Paroles: A Prison Reader.*

Terrie A. Hamazaki of Vancouver has written for the page and the stage. Her stories have appeared in the *Hot & Bothered* series and she has performed her one-act plays at the Fringe Festival and Women in View Performing Arts Festival.

PEGGY HERRING, who divides her time between Victoria and New Delhi, India, has published short fiction in various Canadian literary journals.

CORNELIA C. HORNOSTY lives in Victoria and has published three collections of poetry.

GEORGE K. ILSLEY of Vancouver is the author of *Random Acts of Hatred*, a short story collection. He has been published widely in literary journals.

GAIL JOHNSTON goes back and forth between Vancouver and Lasqueti Island. Her poetry has appeared in *Canadian Literature, Contemporary Verse 2*, and *The Mentor's Canon*.

PATRICK KING was shortlisted for the Chapters/Robertson Davies Prize 1999. He lives in Vancouver.

PATRICK LANE has published more than 20 books of poetry and fiction over a 40-year career, including such recent ones as *Selected Poems 1977-1997, Too Spare, Too Fierce* and *The Bare Plum of Winter Rain*. A winner of the Governor General's Award for poetry, he teaches at the University of Victoria.

JANICE LORE lives in Tofino. Her work has appeared in Canadian literary journals and on CBC Radio. Her first chapbook, *Ipsissima Verba*, was published in 2003.

CAROL MATTHEWS lives on Protection Island. Her short stories have appeared in *Canadian Writers' Journal, Out of Bounds Magazine* and *WordWorks*. She is the editor of *Victor's Verses*, an anthology of dog poetry. Her articles and reviews have appeared in the *National Post*, the *Times Colonist* and *Malahat Review*.

MAUREEN MCCARTHY is the author of four collections of poetry, of which the most recent is *Sneaking through the Evening* (1999). She lives in New Westminster and is a nurse by profession.

JUDY MCFARLANE, whose short fiction has been broadcast on CBC Radio, is at work on a collection of linked stories. A former lawyer, she lives in West Vancouver.

CATHERINE MCNEIL, a teacher, musician and writer, has served as the Fed's Lower Mainland representative. Her work has been anthologized in *Chasing Haley's Comet, Love in the Media Age, All Wound Up* and *Oval Victory* and published in journals such as *The Capilano Review* and *Event*. She lives in Vancouver.

ANNE MILES lives in Gibsons and over the past 25 years has published poetry in journals such as *Quarry, Room of One's Own, Canadian Women's Studies, Herspectives,* and *People's Poetry Letter,* among others. She was a runner-up in the 1997/1998 People's Poem Contest. In addition she has published prose—fiction and articles—in *The Urbanite, Kinesis, Road Rider, Herspectives* and *Venue.*

STEVEN MILLS is a paramedic in Nelson and has had stories published in *New Quarterly, TickleAce, Windsor Review* and *On Spec.* He is a member of SF Canada, the national association of professional speculative fiction writers.

DAN NEIL has published poetry in *Amethyst Review* and won top honours in poetry at the Surrey Writers' Conference. He lives in Langley.

W.H. NEW of Vancouver is a poet and scholar, the former editor of the quarterly *Canadian Literature* and the editor and chief contributor of the massive *Encyclopedia of Literature in Canada.* His is the author of four books of poetry.

A.S. PENNE of Sechelt writes fiction and creative nonfiction. Her first book, *Old Stones,* was published in 2002. Besides teaching English, she facilitates Sechelt's Festival of the Written Arts creative writing workshops for youth.

PAMELA PORTER lives in Sidney and writes narrative poetry for adults and for children.

ROY ROBERTS writes poetry and lives at the ARC (Artists Resource Centre) in Vancouver.

IRENE ROBINSON, one of the Fed's original members, has had many plays produced on the CBC and the BBC. She lives in Vancouver.

LINDA ROGERS, a past president of both the Fed and the League of Canadian Poets, has been awarded the Dorothy Livesay, Milton Acorn and Stephen Leacock prizes in Canada; the Acorn/Rukeyser Award in Canada and the US; the Prix anglais in France; the Voices of Israel Prize; and the Bridport, Cardiff and Kenney awards in Britain. Recent books include *The Bursting Test* (poetry) and *Friday Water* (a novel). She has edited essay collections on the poets P.K. Page, bill bissett and Al Purdy.

TANA RUNYAN lives in Ladner and belongs to the Vancouver writers' group SexDeath&Madness. She has published poetry and non-fiction.

SANDY SHREVE founded and, for the first three years, coordinated BC's Poetry in Transit program. Her most recent poetry collection, *Belonging*, was shortlisted for the Milton Acorn People's Poetry Award. She lives in Vancouver.

JOANNA STREETLY was born in Trinidad and moved to England as a teenager but for the past decade has lived on a floathouse in Clayoquot Sound, where she works as a freelance writer, editor and illustrator.

BETSY TRUMPENER lives "in the bush outside Prince George" and works for CBC Radio, where she produces a feature on writing in the North. She has published in journals such as *Malahat Review*, *Queen Street Quarterly* and *Event*.

ALAN TWIGG, one of the original members of the Fed, is the author of eight books and the publisher of *BC BookWorld*. His most recent book was the poetry collection *Intensive Care*; forthcoming titles include *Belize: A Concise History for Travellers*. He lives in Vancouver.

URSULA VAIRA, who has had poems published in various chapbooks and journals, is also an avid paddler and has pulled many miles among the Gulf Islands, on the west coast of Vancouver Island and along the Inside Passage. She is the publisher of Leaf Press, which publishes poetry chapbooks, and lives in Lantzville.

FERNANDA VIVEIROS, a former community newspaper publisher in Steveston, is a publicist and publishing assistant at Ronsdale Press. She is compiling an anthology of Portuguese-Canadian writing.

Judy Wapp immigrated to Canada from New York in 1968 and in 1971 moved to the West Kootenays. There, in 1991, she was the first person to sign up for Tom Wayman's writing course at the Kootenay School of the Arts.

Betsy Warland's recent books include *Bloodroot: Tracing the Untelling of Motherloss* (lyric prose) and *What Holds Us Here* (poetry). She is a coordinator and mentor in the writing program at Simon Fraser University and lives in Vancouver.

David Watmough has published 16 works of fiction, of which the most recent is *The Moor is Dark Beneath the Moon*. All of them have been written at his home in Vancouver.

Tom Wayman, although he now teaches at the University of Calgary, was raised in Prince Rupert and Vancouver and is especially associated with the literary life of the latter place. His most recent books include *My Father's Cup*, a poetry collection, and *The Dominion of Love*, an anthology of contemporary Canadian love poems that he has edited.

George Whipple was born in Saint John, grew up in Toronto and since 1985 has lived in Burnaby, writing, drawing, and translating French poetry. His most recent poetry collection (his fourth) is *Carousel*.

Elizabeth Rhett Woods has lived in Victoria for many years, is the author of three poetry collections—*Men, Bird Salad* and *Family Fiction*—and two novels, *The Yellow Volkswagen* and *The Amateur*. Her plays and poems have been broadcast on CBC Radio.

Caroline Woodward of Comox is the author of four books, one of which, the short story collection *Disturbing the Peace*, was nominated for the Ethel Wilson Fiction Prize.

Beryl Young of Vancouver is the author of a young adult novel, *Wishing Star Summer*. She has produced recordings for children and has appeared on CBC Radio and television. In 1995 she won the People's Poem Award and was writer-in-residence at Wallace Stegner House in Saskatchewan.